Tales from Grace Chapel Inn®

All in the Timing

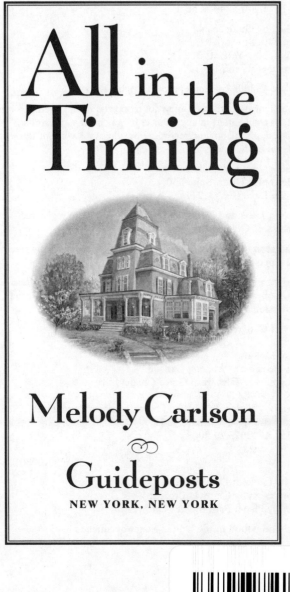

Melody Carlson

Guideposts
NEW YORK, NEW YORK

All in the Timing

ISBN-13: 978-0-8249-4752-1

Published by Guideposts
16 East 34th Street
New York, New York 10016
www.guideposts.com

Distributed by Ideals Publications
535 Metroplex Drive, Suite 250
Nashville, Tennessee 37211

Guideposts, *Ideals* and *Tales from Grace Chapel Inn* are registered
trademarks of Guideposts.

The characters and events in this book are fictional, and any resemblance
to actual persons or events is coincidental.

All Scripture quotations are taken from *The Holy Bible, New International
Version*. Copyright © 1973, 1978, 1984 International Bible Society. Used
by permission of Zondervan Bible Publishers.

Library of Congress Cataloging-in-Publication Data

Carlson, Melody.
  All in the timing / Melody Carlson.
      p. cm. — (Tales from Grace Chapel Inn)
  ISBN 978-0-8249-4752-1
  1. Sisters—Fiction. 2. Bed and breakfast accommodations—Fiction.
  3. Pennsylvania--Fiction. I. Title.
  PS3553.A73257A79 2008
  813'.54—dc22

                                                          2008013844

Cover by Lookout Design Group
Interior design by Cindy LaBreacht
Typeset by Planet Patti Inc. & Nancy Tardi

Printed and bound in the United States of America

10 9 8 7 6 5 4 3 2 1

Chapter  One

Alice paused to admire the vibrant flowerbeds that lined the walk up to Grace Chapel Inn. Bursting with sassy pinks, sunny yellows and rich hues of purple, the spring bulbs that Jane had planted last fall were now a glorious rainbow of color. Springtime was definitely here, with Easter just over a week away.

"Alice," called a voice from the front porch. Alice looked up to see her younger sister Jane garbed in her gardening overalls, tending a large terra-cotta pot of tulips, hyacinths and daffodils. Alice marveled at how her fifty-year-old sister looked years younger with her dark hair gathered in a ponytail.

"Everything looks so beautiful," Alice said as she headed up the stairs. "You've done a fantastic job with the flowers this year, Jane."

"It just keeps getting better, doesn't it?" Jane looked out over her workmanship and smiled.

Alice nodded. "Wouldn't Mother be pleased?"

"It is lovely," said Louise, their older sister, as she stepped out the door and greeted Alice. In her hands was a tray with three tumblers and a crystal pitcher of what appeared to be freshly made lemonade. "It reminds me of how it looked when we were little girls."

"It really does," agreed Alice. "I think Mother's gardening genes are fast at work in our little sister."

Jane smiled, but there was a touch of sadness in her blue eyes. Madeleine Howard had died giving birth to Jane when Alice was twelve and Louise, fifteen.

Louise noticed Jane's expression, for she frowned dramatically at the hole in the knee of Jane's faded overalls and said, "I don't think our mother ever would have worn those kinds of 'gardening jeans.'"

Jane laughed. "Hey, Louise made a pun."

"That's not all I made," said Louise as she held out the pitcher and smiled. "It's such a warm day that I couldn't resist. Do you girls have time?"

"Are you kidding?" said Alice. "Some lemonade would be heavenly. The hospital was so busy that I barely had a moment for a break today. I would love to sit out here and put my feet up for a spell."

"Me too," said Jane. "I'll run inside and wash my hands first. And maybe I'll bring back some oatmeal raisin cookies that I made this morning."

"*Mmm...*," said Alice as she eased herself into the porch swing and ran a hand through her reddish-brown bob. "Don't you just love springtime, Louise?"

Louise nodded as she carefully filled the three glasses, then handed one to Alice. "It is such a time of renewal," she said as she made herself comfortable in the wicker rocker, "as if God is giving all of creation a fresh new start."

Alice sipped the icy lemonade and sighed happily.

Jane rejoined them, setting a plate holding a generous number of cookies on the wicker coffee table. "Did you tell Alice the news yet, Louise?"

Alice reached down for a cookie, then studied Jane's face. She could tell by her sister's expression that something was up.

Louise pushed a strand of her short silver hair from her forehead and cleared her throat. "Mark Graves sent an e-mail to the inn today," she began, waiting, it seemed, for Alice to react. The three sisters had run Grace Chapel Inn in their Victorian home since the death of their father.

Alice took a bite of the cookie and simply nodded. Mark, her college sweetheart, had recently come back into her life. They saw each other occasionally when he was not traveling with his job as chief veterinarian for the Philadelphia Zoo.

"As you know, Mark has a reservation for all next week, from this Saturday through Easter."

Alice nodded again, waiting for Louise to continue, her curiosity beginning to escalate.

"Well, his e-mail today was to request a second room."

"A second room?" echoed Alice.

"Yes," said Jane with raised eyebrows. "What do you think that means?"

"I don't know," admitted Alice.

"He hasn't mentioned anything?" asked Jane.

"No, not a thing," Alice said, turning her attention to Wendell, who was now rubbing himself against her legs. "Does it really matter?"

"Well, isn't Mark coming here to see you?" said Jane. "Why would he suddenly bring someone else along? Does that make any sense?"

"Oh, Jane," said Alice. "I think you're working your brain overtime on this. If Mark requested a second room, I'm sure he has a good reason." She looked at Louise. "Do we have another room? I thought we were all booked."

Louise smiled. "Fortunately for Mark, I had just received

a cancellation. Mark and his mysterious friend will be occupying both the Sunset and the Sunrise rooms."

Of course this inspired Jane to begin singing, rather badly, "Sunrise, sunset . . . sunrise, sunset, quickly flow the years. . . ."

Louise cleared her throat loudly this time. "Please, Jane."

Jane grinned. "It just seemed appropriate. I mean since Mark is coming to see Alice and they might be—"

"I hate to disappoint you, Jane," interrupted Alice, "but it's just a friendly visit. We're certainly not planning to run away and get married, if that's what you're thinking."

"Goodness," said Louise. "I certainly hope not."

Jane smiled as she plucked up another cookie. "Well, that's a relief. Imagine running this inn with only two sisters. It just wouldn't seem right."

"Don't worry," said Alice, winking at Louise. "I'm afraid that, for better or for worse, you two are stuck with me."

Even so, Alice wondered about this mystery guest whom her old beau was bringing to the inn next week. Despite her confident answer to Jane, she was not entirely certain that Mark Graves had the intention of being just friends. But then sisters do not have to tell each other absolutely everything.

Chapter  Two

Friday was Alice's day off, but she got up early as usual, and walked with her friend Vera Humbert, a fifth-grade teacher. Alice spent the rest of the morning working on a quilt that she had been too busy to give attention to the last few months. She planned to take the quilt to Peggy Sanders' baby shower next month, but the busywork was also a good distraction from thoughts of Mark Graves's arrival tomorrow.

"That's looking beautiful," said Jane as she poked her head into Alice's room. "Peggy is going to love it."

"I hope so," said Alice. "Peach and pale green are the colors she chose for the nursery. They work for a boy or a girl."

Jane picked up a section of blocks and admired them. "You're getting really good at this. Sylvia's quilting class must've really helped you."

Alice turned back to her sewing machine to cut a thread. "I'm afraid I've made a few mistakes on it, but the baby won't notice."

"Well, we all have to start somewhere."

Alice nodded. "I've wanted to do a quilting project for a while. It's nice to finally have the time."

"So does it feel good to be on vacation now?"

Alice smiled. "It's wonderful, Jane. I'm so glad you suggested that I take Easter week off."

"You work too hard anyway. Everyone needs to take a break sometimes."

Alice straightened her back, stretching her shoulders. "Perhaps I should take a break now."

"Good idea. I'll see you later," said Jane as she headed off to her room.

Alice went downstairs to the kitchen, then decided to get the mail. She went out the kitchen door and walked to the end of the driveway and the mailbox. She knew that there probably wouldn't be a letter from Mark today, but on the days she wasn't working, she liked to be the first one to get the mail. That way, if there was a letter, she wouldn't have to go through her sisters' questions when they gave it to her later. Sneaky perhaps, but just simpler, she told herself. As expected, there was no letter from him today.

"Hello, Alice." Ethel Buckley waved from her porch as Alice walked back from the mailbox. Ethel, the sisters' aunt, had lived in the inn's carriage house for the past ten years.

"Morning, Auntie," called Alice. "Lovely day, isn't it?"

"Simply beautiful," Ethel called back.

When Alice opened the front door, she saw that Louise had just finished registering new guests.

"I'd like you to meet the Winstons," said Louise. Alice smiled as she was introduced to the attractive middle-aged couple and their pretty teenaged daughter.

"How nice to meet you all," Alice said. "Laura, you must be about sixteen?"

"Laura is seventeen," said the mother, "and a senior."

"What an exciting time of life," said Alice as she studied the girl. Laura's long, chestnut hair was pulled back into a ponytail, and her khaki skirt and navy-and-white striped top were casual but stylish. Although they were indoors, Laura wore a pair of big sunglasses with lime-green frames. More striking than the glasses was the unhappy scowl on her face. It seemed that Laura Winston would rather be anyplace but there.

Alice turned her attention back to the parents. "Will you be in Acorn Hill for long?"

"Laura is on Easter break all next week, so we plan to stay here until next Sunday," said Mrs. Winston. "My parents used to live in Acorn Hill and I've always wanted Laura to see—" She stopped herself and glanced uncomfortably at her daughter. "I mean I've always wanted Laura to experience her grandparents' hometown—"

"Give it a break, Mom," snapped the teen as she tightly folded her arms across her chest.

Alice decided to change the subject. "What was your mother's maiden name, Mrs. Winston? Perhaps we knew your parents."

"Campbell," said Mrs. Winston.

"Eleanor and Roland Campbell?" asked Louise with interest.

"Yes." Mrs. Winston nodded with enthusiasm. "That's right."

"Eleanor and I went to school together," said Louise. "I always liked her. How is she doing?"

"She's fine," said Mrs. Winston.

"Didn't they move to Florida?" asked Alice.

"Yes. That was about fifteen years ago," said Mrs. Winston. "My father had some serious health problems that forced him to retire early. He passed away shortly after they settled down there, but my mother made lots of friends and loves the sunshine. She decided to stay down there. Her condo is near Orlando. In a recent letter she mentioned relatives still living near Acorn Hill."

Mr. Winston picked up the suitcases in an obvious attempt to end this conversation. Just then the phone rang. Louise excused herself and went to the office to answer it.

"May I show you up to your room?" offered Alice, feeling sorry for Mr. Winston. "I'm sure you'd like to get settled."

"Yes, thank you," said Mr. Winston.

Mrs. Winston nodded as she took her daughter's arm. "Your sister said that the roll-away is all set up in there."

Laura made a groaning sound. "Great, I get to spend a whole week sleeping on a cot in my parents' room. What a fun spring break."

Alice laughed as she led them up the stairs. "Yes, I'm sure it will seem rather tame around here, Laura. The teens from our church are having a get-together on Saturday night. Maybe you'd like to—"

"No thanks," said Laura.

"Well, perhaps you'll enjoy getting to know the town," said Alice optimistically, "becoming familiar with the history and whatnot."

"Yes," said Mrs. Winston eagerly. "That's just what I was hoping."

"I'm guessing you're staying in the Garden Room," said Alice when they reached the landing at the top of the stairs. "Since that's the largest room."

"Yes," said Mr. Winston as he waited for Alice to lead the way, "that's what your sister told us."

Alice took them into the spacious room and smiled to see that Jane, as usual, had placed fresh flowers on the bureau as well as in the bathroom. Foil-wrapped homemade chocolates were on the bed pillows, including the one on the roll-away bed that was set up by a window.

"I hope you'll all be very comfortable here," she said as

the three of them entered the room. "Please, let us know if you need anything."

"Thank you," said Mr. Winston as he set a bag on the suitcase stand. He started to reach for his wallet as if to get a tip.

Alice laughed and held up her hand. "You don't need to tip me, Mr. Winston."

He nodded. "Oh, sorry, *um*, thanks."

Alice was on her way out the door when Mrs. Winston called out. "Oh yes, now that I think of it, there is something I need . . . if you have a minute?"

"Yes?" said Alice, turning.

Mrs. Winston nodded to the door. "I'll go downstairs with you." Once they were downstairs, Mrs. Winston told Alice she had a problem.

"Why don't we go to the parlor?" Alice suggested.

After they were seated, Mrs. Winston began to explain. "I really hate to trouble you, Alice," she began, "but, well, you see, Laura is having a very difficult time."

Alice nodded. "Yes, that's not uncommon with teenagers, is it?"

"Yes, well, it's a bit more than just adolescent angst," she continued. "You see, Laura has grown up with juvenile diabetes. Actually diabetes runs in my side of the family. That's what my father died from, or rather complications from the disease."

"Oh, I'm sorry," said Alice. "I'm a nurse and I know how debilitating diabetes can be. But with proper care and nutrition, most diabetics can lead a normal life. I hope that is the case with Laura."

"Up until this year, Laura was doing just fine. She had been diligent with her diet and insulin shots and exercise and, well, everything. In fact, she was such an excellent soccer player that she was even being considered for an athletic scholarship from the local college. We thought that everything was perfectly under control." Mrs. Winston sighed and reached into her pocket for a tissue. "And then it all just fell apart." She dabbed at a stray tear that was streaking down her cheek now.

"I'm so sorry," said Alice as she placed her hand on Mrs. Winston's shoulder. She truly was sorry for this poor woman, but even so, she wondered what she could possibly do to help. "You can be sure I'll tell my sister Jane to have the right kinds of foods on hand for Laura's condition," she added. "Don't worry, Jane knows a lot about nutrition and I will confer with her."

"Thank you," said Mrs. Winston.

"We have several kinds of fruit juice in the refrigerator, in case Laura's blood sugar drops. Please feel free to help yourself to whatever you need from the kitchen. I'll let Jane know about this too."

"Yes," said Mrs. Winston. "I do appreciate that. But what I really wanted to tell you and your sisters is that Laura is blind." She paused to blow her nose.

"Oh my," said Alice. "I am so sorry. I noticed that you held on to her arm, but I thought perhaps that you were steadying yourself. Is her blindness connected to the diabetes? I believe that it's quite rare for anyone to suffer retinopathy at such a young age."

"Yes, you're right, it is. Unfortunately, Laura spent a long weekend at a soccer camp in February, and the schedule was rather demanding. I think Laura was a bit forgetful about her health." She shook her head. "I probably never should've let her go."

"You couldn't know that something would go wrong."

"Perhaps not. Laura overexerted herself and didn't have

her insulin when she needed it, and, of course, with all these kids bringing treats from home, well, Laura ate the wrong kinds of things as well." Mrs. Winston just shook her head.

"Oh dear," said Alice. "That can be very dangerous."

"Yes. It was. Laura ended up in the emergency room. We nearly lost her. She was in a coma for several days and when she came out of it, well . . . her vision was almost completely gone. It has steadily degenerated since then. She can still see shadows sometimes, or so she says, but she is legally blind. Naturally she won't be playing any soccer now."

"Poor thing," said Alice. "No wonder she's so unhappy."

Mrs. Winston nodded. "Yes, I just thought you and your sisters should know how her condition came about. Oh, I suppose it's silly, but I didn't want you to assume that Laura was simply a spoiled brat. She can be quite difficult, but she's still trying to adjust to all that she has lost."

"We wouldn't have thought that, but I am glad you told me."

"And, of course, there's the difficulty in getting around," said Mrs. Winston. "Laura refuses to get a cane or a dog or even to do the most basic training that's been offered to her. I think she's in denial right now. All her friends have been very helpful to her at school. Naturally, her grades have gone down and we may have to consider a special school, which she refuses even to discuss with us."

"Oh, it must be a difficult time for everyone."

"Yes. I suppose I hoped this trip might give us all a break and maybe that something would change. Of course, my husband thinks I'm crazy. He can't understand why I insisted on bringing our blind daughter to a strange place . . ." She paused and looked close to tears again. "Maybe he's right."

"Oh no," said Alice as she patted Mrs. Winston's hand. "I think it's a wonderful idea to come to Acorn Hill. Who knows what might happen here? I usually work part-time as a nurse at the hospital in Potterston, but I've taken the week off, so I hope you'll feel free to call on me if you need anything. I will try to do whatever I can to help Laura feel right at home."

"Thank you, Alice."

"I'll let my sisters know about everything," she assured her.

"Well, I feel much better now." Mrs. Winston smiled. "Perhaps you're right. Who knows what might happen?"

"Yes," said Alice. "I believe that God really does work in mysterious ways. I think that by the time you leave next week, things will be looking up."

"Oh, I hope so."

After the two women parted, Alice went off in search of her sisters. She found them on the back porch, with their backs to her. They were discussing whether to plant the geraniums that Jane had started in the sunroom.

"I think it is far too soon," said Louise with authority. "We might still get frost."

"I can watch the weather forecast," said Jane in a slightly irritated voice. "I'll cover them if necessary. I'm just so tired of looking at those empty flower boxes outside the kitchen and I—"

"Excuse me," said Alice.

"Oh, I didn't hear you," said Jane as she pushed a dark strand of hair from her face. "We were just trying to decide about—"

"Yes, I heard your discussion." Alice suppressed a grin. "And just for your information, I will not act as a tie-breaker in this little dispute."

Jane laughed. Louise smiled, then said, "Thank you for taking care of the Winstons for me. That was a very aggravating phone call. A gentleman from Pittsburgh wanted to make reservations for Easter weekend, and even though I told him we were booked full, he just would not give up. Then he asked about Memorial Day weekend, and once again I had to tell him we were full. Well, he started getting quite irate with me."

"You should've told him that we'll never have room for him," said Jane.

"I tried to keep my patience," said Louise. "Finally he asked about a weekend in August that was open, but, to be perfectly honest, I wanted to tell him that it was booked too."

Alice chuckled. "So did you go ahead and make his reservation?"

Louise nodded.

"So when exactly is Mr. Sourpuss coming?" asked Jane. "I think I'll make sure to be out of town that weekend."

Louise gave her youngest sister the look—the look that she had been giving Jane since she was a little girl—the look that meant "don't even think about it."

"Well, maybe we should just put up a sign," suggested Jane. "You know, like they have in restaurants: 'We have the right to refuse service.'"

"That certainly wouldn't be hospitable," said Louise.

"Especially for an inn that's called Grace Chapel," added Alice.

"I suppose you're right," said Jane.

"Speaking of disgruntled guests," said Alice as she closed the door between the porch and the kitchen. "I need to tell you about Laura Winston."

"My goodness," said Louise. "I don't think that I have ever seen such an unfriendly teenager. If I were her mother I would—"

"You don't understand," said Alice, then she quickly explained the situation in detail.

"Oh, the poor thing," said Jane. "That's so sad. To become

blind at any age is a tragedy, but at seventeen? Just when life is beginning to unfold."

Louise shook her head. "I had no idea. Goodness, I feel so bad having judged her."

"I did the exact same thing myself," admitted Alice.

"Well, we must do everything we can to make her stay here as pleasant as possible," said Jane.

"Yes," said Alice. "I told Mrs. Winston that Laura would be in good hands here."

"How about the teen thing?" asked Jane. "Laura might enjoy meeting some new—"

"I already mentioned it to her," said Alice. "She wasn't interested."

"Oh."

"I suppose someone else could invite her again," said Alice. "It might be the kind of situation where we need to be persistent to get—"

"Yoo-hoo," called a familiar voice.

"Hi, Aunt Ethel," said Jane.

"What's going on here?" asked Ethel. "Some kind of secret sister meeting?"

"No," said Louise. "Alice was just giving us some information about a guest."

Ethel's eyebrows lifted. "Oh my. Certainly my nieces are not gossiping, are you?"

"Not gossip," said Alice, then Louise explained the situation with Laura.

"Dear me," said Ethel. "That's too bad."

"So, we've decided that we should try to reach out to her," said Alice. "Maybe one of us can break through to her before the week is up."

"Speaking of guests," said Ethel, turning her attention to

Alice, "when is that handsome animal doctor showing up here?"

Alice felt her cheeks growing warm. "Not until tomorrow," she told Ethel. "His last letter said he expects to be here late Saturday night." She suddenly turned to Louise. "That is, unless that has changed too. Did he mention—"

"I don't recall him mentioning a change in his arrival time," said Louise.

"So what else has changed?" asked Ethel.

"Why don't we go inside," suggested Jane as she opened the door into her kitchen. "It's getting a little crowded out here."

As soon as they were in the kitchen, Louise told Ethel about Mark's mystery guest and once again all attention was back on Alice.

"Who do you think it is?" asked Ethel.

Alice just shrugged. "I don't have a clue."

Just then, they heard the bell in the foyer ding, and Louise excused herself. "That's probably the Langleys," she said as she hurried out.

"A full house this week?" asked Ethel.

"That's right," said Jane as she put on the teakettle. "Tea, anyone?"

"Do you have any of those delicious ginger biscotti left?" asked Ethel hopefully.

Jane grinned as she produced the cookie jar and peeked inside. "Lucky for you, there are just enough left for a little tea party."

Chapter Three

Alice had offered to put away the tea things while Jane made a quick run to the grocery store and Louise went off to search for a heating pad for Mr. Langley. The poor man had strained his back loading his wife's luggage into the trunk of their car and had been in pain the whole three hours that it took them to drive to Acorn Hill. Alice had promptly prescribed treatments of alternate hot and cold packs, along with ibuprofen and rest.

"Send me your bill later," the elderly man had teased her as Louise and his wife helped him to make his way slowly up the stairs.

"Just remember, I'm not a doctor," said Alice. "I hope that I won't wish that I had malpractice insurance."

"I don't put much stock in doctors anyway," said Mr. Langley.

"Well, I'm sure that you'll be feeling much better by tomorrow," Alice assured him.

Now Alice hummed to herself as she puttered about Jane's cheerful kitchen. A real departure from the antiques and the more formal feeling of the rest of the house, Jane's bright, paprika-colored cabinets, perky curtains and black and white checkerboard tile floors always made Alice happy. Just as she was hanging up the dishtowel, she heard the familiar ding of the bell in the foyer.

She removed her apron and patted her hair in place. It was still a day early for Mark and his friend to be arriving, but, on the other hand, no other guests were expected at the inn. When she entered the foyer, she saw a young man looking up at the high ceiling. He seemed out of place. In fact, he was a rather untidy young man with shaggy blond hair and oversized pants that appeared to be almost falling off his narrow hips.

"May I help you?" she asked with a smile.

"Yeah," he said, looking over his shoulder uncomfortably. "I think I'm supposed to be here, at this inn, you know. I mean I'm supposed to be meeting someone here."

"Are you here with Dr. Mark Graves?" she asked.

He nodded. "Yeah, sort of. I mean he told me to meet him here. Is he here yet?"

"No. I don't believe he is arriving until tomorrow evening." She held out her hand. "I'm Alice Howard. My sisters and I run this inn."

He shook her hand, then quickly pulled his away. "Yeah, right. I'm Adam. Adam Peterson."

She could tell that he did not recognize her name. *But then*, she thought, why *should he? Why would Mark have bothered to tell this young man about her?* "So are you going to be staying here?" she asked. "In the inn, I mean. I was told that Dr. Graves was bringing a friend and—"

"Yeah, I guess so," he said quickly. "Mark told me to meet him here and I was going to spend time with him next week. I thought he said to come today. Am I too early or something?"

"No, no," she said. "You're fine. Your room is all ready for you. Would you like me to show you up now?" she offered.

"Yeah," he said. "That'd be cool."

"Do you have any bags?" she asked.

He hoisted a dusty black backpack over his shoulder. "This is it."

"Okay, then I'll take you up."

"That's all right," he said, after glancing up the stairs. "You can just give me the key and tell me where it is. You don't have to go up there or anything."

"Oh, it's no trouble," she said as she headed up the stairs ahead of him. She hated to admit it to herself, but something about this young man bothered her. She did not want to judge him, but his manner made her uncomfortable.

"How long have you known Dr. Graves?" she asked him after they reached the top of the stairs.

He shrugged, then turned his attention to Wendell, who was happily warming himself in a shaft of sunshine. "Oh, like forever, you know. He's been around since I was a baby." He set aside his backpack as he knelt to pet the cat.

Alice smiled. "Friend of the family?"

"Yeah, I guess you could say that." His back remained to her as he continued to stroke Wendell.

It seemed fairly clear that Adam was not about to divulge any unnecessary information, so Alice opened the door to the Sunset Room and simply said, "This is your room." She had already decided that Mark should have the Sunrise Room, since it was the room that she had decorated . . . with some help from Jane. It seemed logical that his friend should have the room just across the hall.

"This is nice," Adam said as he looked around.

"I hope you'll be comfortable." Alice went through the information about when they served breakfast, that there were restaurants in town for other meals, but that he and Mark were invited to have dinners with the sisters.

"Where's the TV?" he asked as he dropped his backpack to the floor with a loud thump.

"I'm sorry," she said. "We don't have televisions in the inn. We like to provide a quiet place for our guests to relax and unwind. We do have a library downstairs from which you are free to borrow books, and my sister Louise occasionally plays piano in the evenings . . ." She could tell by his expression that this did not impress him in the least.

"Yeah, okay," he said. "Whatever."

She forced another smile as she made her way to the door. "Well, make yourself at home and let us know if you need anything."

He nodded, but just continued to stand there in the middle of the room as if he had no idea how he had gotten there or why he had come. It was, in fact, a mystery to Alice too. She asked herself, who was this young man and what did he have to do with Mark Graves? She tried to push these questions from her mind as she made her way downstairs.

"Hello, Alice," said Mrs. Winston as she and her husband met Alice at the bottom of the stairs. "We're going out for a walk just now."

Alice looked at the couple as they headed toward the door. "Laura's not joining you?" she asked.

Mrs. Winston sadly shook her head. "She said she wants to take a nap."

"She sleeps too much," said Mr. Winston as he opened the door. "Some fresh air would probably do her good."

"Well, we can't very well force her, dear," said Mrs. Winston.

"Have a nice walk," said Alice, feeling sorry about the stress that this couple seemed to be experiencing.

"I'm back," called Jane from the kitchen.

Alice went in and offered to help unload groceries.

"Thanks," said Jane.

"How about if I bring them in from the car and you can start putting them away," said Alice, "since you do a better job at fitting everything in place than I do."

"Sounds like a plan," said Jane as she put a jug of milk into the refrigerator.

Alice finally brought the last bag from the car and then sat down at the table to watch as Jane continued to put things away. "We got a new guest while you were out," said Alice as Jane filled a large ceramic bowl with apples.

"Really?" Jane turned and looked at her. "Is it Mark?"

Alice shook her head. "Guess again."

"Mark's mysterious friend?" Jane balanced the last apple on top.

"What is this about Mark's friend?" asked Louise as she came into the kitchen. "Have they arrived already?"

"Not *they*," said Alice. "Mark's friend is here. At least I think he's Mark's friend. To be honest, I felt a bit confused."

"Why is that?" asked Louise.

"I'm not sure. But something about him seemed, well, a bit odd." Alice shook her head. "Perhaps I'm just imagining things. I don't know."

"*Who* is Mark's friend?" demanded Jane.

"He's a young man named Adam Peterson," said Alice.

"A *young* man?" Louise frowned. "How young?"

"I didn't ask, but I'm guessing maybe college age. I'm not sure."

"Do you know what his relationship is to Mark?" asked Louise.

Alice took an apple from the bowl and went to the sink to wash it off. "He said he's known Mark his whole life." His sister doesn't have a son named Adam. So he's not Mark's nephew."

"No, that's right," Alice said, then took a bite of the apple.

Jane's eyebrows shot up. "Maybe he's Mark's long-lost son!"

"Son? How can that be?" Louise asked. "Mark Graves has never been married."

"Well, you don't—"

"Jane," said Alice. "Mark has never mentioned any son."

"Well, I'm reading a novel about a young man who is searching for his birth father and he's—"

"That is exactly why you should read something besides fiction," Louise said. "Goodness knows how it fills your head with strange ideas."

Alice chuckled. "Well, I'm reading a murder mystery, Louise. Do you think I might become dangerous?"

"*Harrumph*," Louise said, giving Alice an exasperated look.

"Well, what was this young man like?" asked Jane. "You said his name was Adam?"

"Yes," said Alice. "To be honest, he seemed unhappy."

"Well, that is about right," said Louise. "We already have a depressed teenager and a guest who is suffering with a bad back. Why should we not have an unhappy young man as well?"

"Won't we be the jolly bunch for Easter week," said Jane as she put several pounds of butter into the refrigerator.

"Remember," said Alice. "Part of our mission in this inn has always been to help people. Maybe that's what this week will be about."

"You are absolutely right," said Louise.

"I'm still curious," said Jane. "I'd like to know what Adam has to do with Mark Graves. And why it was so important for them to spend this week together when everyone knows that the only reason Mark is coming back to Acorn Hill is to see Alice."

"Oh, Jane," said Alice. "Mark is coming here because he really likes our town and wants to—"

"Go on, Alice," said Jane, waving a hand at her older sister as she took a bite out of her own apple. "You can go ahead and act as if there's nothing between you and Mark if you like. But I'm not buying it."

Alice dropped her apple core into the trash and just shrugged. "I guess only time will tell."

Jane nodded as she chewed and finally said, "Yep, Alice. That's exactly what I'm counting on."

Just then they heard a loud crash from the direction of the foyer.

"Oh dear!" cried Louise.

The three sisters hurried out to see what was wrong.

"Oh, Laura," exclaimed Alice when she found the girl squatting in front of the shattered pieces of a broken ceramic vase that had held a flower arrangement. She took Laura's hand in her own. "You've cut yourself."

"I'm sorry," said Laura, pulling her hand away. "I shouldn't have come down by myself. I just thought that—"

"Don't worry," said Alice as she gently helped the girl to her feet. "Be careful of the wet floor, I'm sure it's slippery." She moved the girl out of harm's way. "I'm a nurse and I can take care of that cut for—"

"That's right," Jane assured her. "I'm Alice's sister Jane, and speaking from experience, there's no one better than Alice to bandage a cut."

Laura turned her head toward the sound of Jane's voice. "I—I'm sorry if I made a mess," she muttered. "I ran into something, I think a table maybe. I'd just come downstairs. I was trying to pick it up and—"

"Hey, no problem," said Jane. "I never really liked that vase anyway."

"That's true enough," said Louise with a frown since it had been her vase. "I'm Louise, dear. Don't worry, Jane and I will have it cleaned up before you know it."

"Come on," Alice urged Laura. "Let's go to the bathroom and wash out your cut. I don't think you need stitches, but I want to be sure."

As Alice attended to the cut, which did not need stitches, she said, "It must be hard getting used to not having your sight."

Laura sighed loudly, but said nothing.

Alice continued to talk as she cleaned the wound. "When someone loses the ability to do something they once loved, it seems they must go through a period of grieving."

"Grieving?"

"Yes, as if someone you loved had died. You have to work through the stages. For instance, you might've felt some denial at first."

Laura nodded.

"You tell yourself that it's not really happening."

"Yeah."

"And then you feel guilt." Alice began to wrap Laura's hand in gauze.

"Like it was my fault that I lost my vision?"

"That's right."

"Yeah, well, I guess I felt that too. Like if I'd been more careful with my insulin and stuff, things might've gone differently. But it's still not fair. I mean other kids don't have to put up with this kind of crud!"

"And then you get angry—"

"That's right!" snapped Laura. "And that's how I feel right now." She held up her bandaged hand. "Like this! This never would've happened before. It's just so stupid and sense-less! I don't see why God allows stuff like this to happen to anyone."

"That's a natural reaction," said Alice as she finished with the last bit of tape.

"Really?" Laura seemed somewhat soothed.

"Yes." Alice snapped the first-aid box closed. "But you just don't want to stay in that angry stage for too long, Laura. You want to move on."

"What if I can't?"

Alice pushed a strand of hair from Laura's eyes. "You must ask God to help you."

Laura stood up, looking unconvinced. She thanked Alice for her help and fumbled to find the door.

"Let me get that," said Alice.

Just as they emerged from the bathroom, Mr. and Mrs. Winston were entering the inn.

"Oh no!" exclaimed Mrs. Winston when she saw the white bandage. "What happened to your hand, Laura?"

After Alice quickly explained, Laura asked her mother to help take her back to their room.

"I thought you were going to take a nap, Laura," said Mr. Winston as the three of them went upstairs. "If you had wanted to walk around, you should've come with us."

"Oh, don't pick on her," said Mrs. Winston. "It's plain to see she changed her mind. Does it hurt much, honey?"

"No, it's fine," said Laura in an irritated tone. "I wish you wouldn't freak every time something happens, Mom."

Alice paused in the parlor to say a silent prayer for the Winstons before she headed back into the kitchen to help Jane with dinner. Suddenly, she suspected this week was not going to be easy for anyone at Grace Chapel Inn.

Chapter  Four

A lice dropped the last pieces of pared potato into a pot of water and then rinsed off the peeler. "Anything else?" she asked her sister.

"No, that should do it." Jane grinned. "It's so nice that you don't mind doing things like peeling potatoes or chopping vegetables. It's very helpful to have a good prep cook."

Alice laughed. "Is that what I am?"

"Sure. If you ever get tired of nursing and still need a job, I'll be happy to give you a good recommendation. Good prep cooks can be hard to come by."

"I'll keep that in mind."

"Have you seen anything of Mark's young friend this afternoon?" asked Jane as she measured the seasoning mix that she had made for her special roast chicken. Jane's roast chicken was so tender and flavorful that Alice and Louise looked forward to the occasions when Jane served this homey dish.

"I don't think he's come downstairs at all," said Alice as she put the lid on the seasoning and returned it to the spice cupboard. "I was hoping that he would. I wanted to talk to him some more. He seems so somber. I thought that I might interest him in reading something. Perhaps that book about hiking the Appalachian Trail that Mr. Stefan left for our library. Adam looks as if he might like the outdoors and he certainly could use some laughs. I remember Mr. Stefan saying that it was a very funny book. I must admit that I felt bad when I saw how disturbed Adam was by our not having televisions for the guests."

Jane chuckled. "Well, to the younger generation, it is fairly disturbing." She glanced up at her small black-and-white TV, which was tucked into the cabinet. "Sometimes I think I might get a little loopy if I couldn't catch up on the latest news."

"But you hardly ever turn it on," observed Alice.

"Yes, but I know that I can, and that makes all the difference."

"Perhaps we should have another TV, somewhere in the inn, one that doesn't actually work. Then maybe our young guests would feel reassured just to see it."

"Ha," said Jane. "You could be onto something."

"Hello," said Louise as she joined them. "Oh good, roast chicken."

Jane smiled as she basted the golden meat and a delicious aroma filled the kitchen. "It's not fancy, but it's good."

"Alice," said Louise in a lowered voice, "I thought you should know that your young man is wandering about the inn."

Alice felt her eyebrows lifting. "My young man?"

"Oh, you know what I mean." Louise frowned. "I realize that he is a guest, but he looks rather, well, unkempt."

Jane laughed. "That's just the way kids dress, Louie."

"Have you seen him?" demanded Louise.

"Well, no . . ."

Alice cleared her throat. "Louise is right, Jane. Adam carries the sloppy look to an extreme."

"Yes," agreed Louise. "I think you should go and check on him, Alice."

"*Check* on him?" Even though Alice agreed with Louise about Adam's appearance, she did not care for the insinuation. "Why exactly do you think I should check on him, Louise?"

"Maybe she's afraid he's going to steal the family silver," teased Jane as she adjusted the low flame under the covered pot holding the potatoes.

"No," said Louise. "I don't think he is a thief, but as I said there is something about him, Alice. Something doesn't feel right to me. It occurs to me that we have allowed him into our house without knowing a single thing about him. Goodness, it could turn out that he is not even associated with Mark Graves. You told me that you had mentioned Mark's name to him when he arrived. Adam could have just picked up on what you were assuming."

"Oh, I don't think . . ."

"But you don't know either," finished Louise. "And I, for one, would appreciate it if someone kept an eye on him. At least until Mark arrives."

"Oh, Louise," said Jane. "Surely, you don't expect Alice to keep him under surveillance. Seriously, what do you think he's going to do?"

"I don't know. All I know is that he makes me uncomfortable in my own home."

"All right," said Alice. "Don't worry about it anymore, Louise. I shall go and keep our young man company." Alice left the kitchen, feeling glad to get away from Louise's suspicions.

The truth was, however, that Alice found Adam to be unsettling and she was very eager to learn what his connection could possibly be to Mark. Despite herself, she had considered the possibility that Jane had suggested. What if Adam was indeed Mark's son? It was possible, but she sincerely hoped that it was not true.

Alice discovered Adam in the library. *Handy,* she thought, since she wanted to recommend some books. "Hello, Adam," she said as she entered the room.

He quickly replaced a small bronze statue that a parishioner had given her father many years ago and turned around without saying anything.

"I thought I could suggest some books for you," she said, ignoring the young man's lack of manners.

He shrugged and looked away.

"I thought that you might be bored without television and I recalled a book—"

"I'm not interested in reading," he said quickly. "I did enough of that in school."

"So you're not in school now?" she asked.

He just shook his head and moved over to where her father's old chess set was sitting on a side table.

"I assume that you must be out of high school," she continued as she fluffed a sofa cushion.

"Yeah," he said as he picked up the black king and examined it more closely.

"Do you play chess?" she asked.

He just shrugged again. "A little."

"I enjoy playing chess," she told him. "Would you like to—"

"Look, lady . . ." He set the chess piece back in its place and turned to her. "I don't expect you to entertain me or anything. I'm mostly just killing time until Mark gets here. I might not even stay, you know. I just have some business to take care of with him. So, don't worry about me, okay? I can take care of myself." Then, before she could respond, he walked out of the room.

She followed him out to the foyer, wishing for something kind and gracious to say to him in response to his rudeness, but all she could think was that this young man needed a course in manners and etiquette. If he was any relation to Mark Graves, she would be very surprised. In fact, she was beginning to understand Louise's concern. What if this young man was a complete stranger and he had simply taken advantage of her assumption that he was a friend of Mark's?

She decided to ask him now about the specifics of his relationship with Mark, but it was too late. He was already out the front door. She looked out the window in time to see him getting into the dilapidated old Nissan that was parked on the street in front of the inn. With a squeal of tires he took off.

"Oh my!" she said aloud.

"You see," said Louise as she came out of the living room and joined Alice. "Something is not right with that young man."

"I'll admit that his manners could use improving," said Alice, "but I think it's unfair to judge him. I'm sure that Mark will make things clear when he arrives tomorrow."

"Well," said Louise. "I just hope he doesn't kill us in the middle of the night."

"Louise!" said Alice.

"I'm not serious, sister," said Louise with a twinkle in her blue eyes. "On the other hand, I may ask Jane to hide the family silver."

Alice just shook her head; it was too late to respond since the Winstons were just coming down the stairs.

"We're off to dinner," said Mrs. Winston. "We have reservations at that nice-looking restaurant downtown."

"Oh, you must mean Zachary's."

"Yes, that's it."

"Have a lovely evening," said Louise.

Alice noticed that Laura had on a pair of hot pink sunglasses that matched her sweater top. "How's your hand, Laura?"

Laura held up the bandaged hand and shrugged. "It throbs a little, but I guess it's okay."

"Maybe you should let me check it when you get back from dinner," suggested Alice. "We wouldn't want any infection to set in."

"That's a good idea," said Mrs. Winston.

"Enjoy your dinner," said Alice as she closed the front door behind them.

"Poor child," said Louise. "Her blindness must be so hard on her."

Alice nodded. "I'm really praying for a breakthrough for her."

"I had better go help Jane," said Louise. "I'm going to take some dinner up to the Langleys since he is still laid up with his back."

"That's nice of Jane to offer them dinner," said Alice. "Let me help you with it."

It was not long before the Langleys were all set, and it turned out that Mr. Langley absolutely adored roast chicken. "Guess it's not so bad being laid up," he said as Alice arranged the tray on his bed for him.

"Well, you certainly picked the right place to recover,"

said Louise as she handed him a cloth napkin. "Between my sister the gourmet cook and my sister the registered nurse, you could hardly be in better hands."

"Bless all three of you," said Mrs. Langley as she sat down at the small table on which Louise had set her tray. "This looks delicious."

By the time they got downstairs, Jane had the kitchen table set and ready for dinner. "I was about to ring the dinner bell," she said as they came and sat down.

"Well, the guests are all taken care of," said Louise after a short blessing had been said. "So, I guess we can just relax for a while."

"All the guests?" asked Jane as she passed the mashed potatoes to Alice. "What is our young man doing for dinner tonight?"

"I have no idea," said Alice. "When he arrived, I told him that he and Mark were invited to dinner, but he didn't indicate if he'd join us."

"Well, he certainly took off in a huff," said Louise. "I'm sure that half of Acorn Hill heard his tires squealing down the street."

Jane laughed. "That's what that noise was?"

"He's not a very thoughtful young man," said Louise as she buttered her roll. "I will be very interested to hear what his relationship is to Mark Graves. If you ask me, those two are as different as night and day. I am almost positive that they are of no relation whatsoever."

"He seems troubled," said Alice as she took a portion of cooked carrots with butter and dill sauce.

"*Humph*," said Louise. "At least he has his sight."

"There's an idea," said Alice suddenly. "Maybe I should introduce Adam to Laura and see if—"

"No, Alice!" said Louise vehemently.

"Why not?" asked Jane.

"Really," said Louise, "it would be wrong to introduce that young girl to the influence of that surly, not to mention unkempt, young man. I won't hear of it. We have a responsibility to our guests, Alice. We cannot simply hand Laura over to Adam because we assume that he is an acquaintance of Mark's."

Alice frowned. Louise sometimes took her role as the eldest a bit too seriously. "But, Louise," Alice said. "It might be good for both of them."

"I think it's a bad idea," Louise insisted, "a very bad idea. For one thing, consider Laura's parents . . . how would they feel if we exposed their daughter to a questionable young man like that?"

"How do we know he's questionable?" asked Alice.

"I know that we shouldn't judge people on appearances, but just look at him and you must admit that all is not right," said Louise. "Then there is the way he talks to you. Good grief, he won't look anyone directly in the eye."

"Louise may be right," said Jane. "I hate to judge him, but until Mark gets here, we really don't know much about him. It might be a mistake to encourage a friendship with Laura. Think about it, Alice. She is very vulnerable right now and it's clear that she has her own issues to deal with. We don't want to create any unnecessary problems for her or her parents."

Alice nodded. "I suppose you could be right."

"She *is* right," said Louise. "It just would not be prudent."

Jane suddenly pointed her fork at Alice. "I'm just dying to know what Adam has to do with Mark. Does Mark have a cell phone or some way that we could reach him, Alice? Do you think he's checking his e-mail?"

Alice shrugged. "He has a cell phone, but I don't have the number. I use his work or his home number. I don't know how often he checks his e-mail."

"Well," said Louise, "I think I would sleep better tonight if I knew that Adam really is a trustworthy young man."

"Oh, Louise." Alice was feeling unusually exasperated tonight. "Do you honestly think Mark would send some criminal to stay in our inn?"

"Not at all," said Louise. "I am only concerned that Adam may have nothing to do with Mark at all."

Jane laughed. "Yes, perhaps he's an impostor. Maybe he got rid of the real Adam Peterson and has taken his identity."

"I'm not joking," said Louise. "Until we know for sure who this young man is, we should exercise caution."

"Oh." Alice could think of no other response to that. The more she considered it, the more she wondered if her sisters' scenarios could have merit. *But,* she thought, *even if Adam isn't who he says he is, what can I do about it now?*

Chapter  Five

After the Winstons had returned from dinner, Alice examined Laura's wound and put on another sterile bandage. Then she decided to retire to her room to work on her quilt. She tinkered at it for a couple of hours, but the results seemed paltry compared to the efforts. After sewing the downside of the fabric up and having to pick apart the seam, she decided to set the project aside.

She put on her cozy blue pajamas, then made herself comfortable in her easy chair. She had recently purchased a new paperback book from Nine Lives Bookstore. It was a newly released mystery from one of her favorite writers, but after just a few pages she found herself, once again, distracted and unable to focus. She finally closed the book and sighed.

Was this strange uneasiness due to Mark's impending visit to the inn? Goodness, it had not been that long since she had last seen him, and they had kept in touch in the meantime. Why should she feel so unsettled now? Perhaps she was just worried about the young man, whom both her sisters seemed to dislike. To be honest, Alice was not fond of Adam herself. If he was a friend of Mark's, should she try to think of him as a friend of hers? She picked up her book again, telling herself to just let these things go for the night, but she could not.

Finally, she gave up and decided to go downstairs to fix some cocoa. A mug of warm cocoa usually helped her to relax and eventually to sleep. She had made the cocoa and was tiptoeing with it back through the darkened inn when she heard voices coming from the library. Curious about who was in there at that hour, she decided to investigate.

As she approached the door to the library, she determined that the voices belonged to Laura Winston and Adam Peterson. Despite her earlier idea about getting these two young people together, she felt seriously alarmed now. Questions ran through her mind. *What are they doing down here? Are they alone? Do Laura's parents know where she is? How did Laura find her way down here in the first place?*

"So how long have you been blind?" Alice heard Adam ask.

"A couple of months," she said.

"And you can't see *anything*? "

"Shadows, sometimes."

"And it's not going to get better?"

"I don't know . . ."

"Well, that's a bummer, all right."

"Yeah, tell me about it."

"*Laura?*" a woman's voice called out in a whisper, yet Alice could hear the sound of worry in it. It came from upstairs, and Alice knew it was Mrs. Winston calling. She hurried to the foot of the stairs to reassure the woman.

"Down here," called Alice quietly.

Mrs. Winston, wearing a pink satin robe, peered over the railing with a troubled expression. "Pardon?"

"Laura's down here," Alice mouthed the words, pointing in the direction of the library.

Within seconds, Mrs. Winston was at Alice's side. "Is she all right?"

"Yes," whispered Alice. "She's fine."

"But how did she get down here?"

"I don't know. She's talking to another guest in the library just now."

"We had fallen asleep, but when I got up for a drink of water, I saw that Laura was gone." She still looked frightened. "I didn't know what to think."

"Mom?" Just then Laura came out of the library, using the hallway wall to guide her. "Is that you?"

"Yes, dear." Mrs. Winston went over and took Laura's arm. "What are you doing down here?"

"I couldn't sleep," she said. "I didn't want to disturb you, so I went out on the landing and Adam was out there. And, well, we just started talking and stuff and he thought it'd be better to go downstairs so we wouldn't wake anyone."

"I see." Mrs. Winston nodded, but her expression was troubled. "Well, it's late, Laura. I think both you and, uh, Adam should call it a night." She glanced in the direction of the library, but Adam did not seem to wish to make an appearance.

"Good night," said Alice. "Sleep well."

"Thank you," said Mrs. Winston. "I'm sorry if we disturbed you."

"Not at all," she assured them. "I was still up." Then, as they went upstairs, she went to the library to check on Adam. "It's rather late," she told him, hoping it did not sound too much like a scolding, although it was meant to be a hint.

"Yeah, I couldn't sleep."

"Yes, I heard that, but Laura's mother was quite worried about her. You probably should check with the Winstons before you, uh, well, before you spend any time with Laura."

"Why's that?" he asked in a belligerent voice.

"Because they're both very concerned for Laura. She has only been blind a short while and—"

"I know all about that," he said.

"She doesn't really have the skills to get around yet," continued Alice, no longer caring if she sounded like she was scolding or not. "In fact, she ran into a table earlier today and actually cut her—"

"I know about that too." He stood now and, without even looking at her, headed for the door.

"I'm just saying you should check with her parents before—"

"Yeah, yeah," he said as he exited. "I heard what you said."

"Well, good night, Adam."

He just kept on walking down the hall and then up the stairs without bothering to say good night to her. Well! she thought, as she turned off the light in the library and headed back up to her room. By the time she got there, her cocoa was tepid and unappealing. She took a few sips of the luke-warm liquid, then decided to go to bed.

Before she fell asleep, she prayed for both Adam and Laura. Surely they both had problems and needed some divine help. Then she prayed for herself.

Please, heavenly Father, she prayed. *Give me an extra-large dose of patience for that young man. Because the truth is, I would like to wring his neck. I'm sorry about that. Please, forgive me, and help me to be gracious and kind. Amen.*

To her surprise, she slept relatively well that night,

though she felt nervous and unsettled the following morning. Just the same, she adhered to her regular Saturday routine, putting on her jeans, sweatshirt and walking shoes, then heading over to Vera Humbert's for their morning walk.

"You seem troubled," said Vera after they had barely gone one block. "What's the problem?" Vera and Alice had been friends for years and were very sensitive to each other's moods.

Alice frowned. "I'm not entirely sure."

"Worried about Mark coming today?" Vera asked gently.

"Yes," she admitted. "I guess I'm not certain . . ."

"About what?"

"Oh, you know," said Alice. "About us, I suppose. I'm not sure what our relationship is going to be . . . what it should be."

"What do you think Mark expects?"

"I don't know. The idea of marriage came up once, but we haven't discussed it seriously. "

"What does he talk about in his letters?"

"He mostly writes about his work, and if he says anything concerning us and our relationship, it's more about our friendship and how much he appreciates it. Oh, and a few other things, I suppose." Alice was not sure that she wanted to tell even her best friend *everything*.

"And how does that make you feel?"

Alice shrugged.

"Well, what do you want from the relationship, Alice?" Vera had stopped walking now and was looking right into her eyes.

"I don't know, Vera. I really don't." Alice sighed. "And there's a complication."

"A complication?"

"Yes." Alice told her about Adam and even confessed that she disliked the young man. "And that's just not like me," she continued. "You know me, Vera, I try to see the good in everyone. But there's something about Adam that just sets my teeth on edge. Louise can barely tolerate him. And, Jane, well, she's trying to be patient, but I can tell that even she's feeling concerned."

"Oh my." Vera shook her head, then they continued walking. "That is quite a complication. But, tell me, what exactly is Adam's relationship to Mark?"

"I have no idea. All I know is that Adam has known Mark all his life."

"Maybe Adam's a relative. A nephew perhaps?"

"I know Mark's only sister and Adam is not her child."

Vera considered this. "Do you think Adam could be . . ." Then she stopped herself. "No, that's ridiculous."

"If you were wondering if he might be Mark's son, you're not alone. Jane has already suggested that possibility. As far as I know, Mark has never been married," Alice paused, "but Mark and I have only been reacquainted for such a short time . . . after so many years. It's possible that I don't know everything about him."

"No, I think we're on the wrong track there." said Vera quickly. "Sorry, Alice. I shouldn't have suggested such a thing."

Alice nodded. "Yes, it does seem rather unlikely."

"Well," said Vera as they paused on the curb for the morning traffic to move along. "You do have your work cut out for you this week, my friend."

Alice sighed. "Yes, that's what I'm thinking too."

They spent the rest of their walk making final plans for the annual Easter egg hunt that Grace Chapel had scheduled for next Saturday. As usual, it would be held in the city park. Vera had already placed the notice in the newspaper that all residents of Acorn Hill were invited to attend. By the time they reached the inn, their parting place, they had just about covered everything.

"Whose car is that?" asked Vera as they paused on the sidewalk to say good-bye.

Alice followed Vera's gaze over to where Adam's dilapidated Nissan was parked. Sporting three different colors of paint, the small vehicle had a dented front fender and a missing taillight, and duct tape appeared to be the only thing keeping the trunk closed. "That's Adam's car," she told Vera.

"Looks like this young man is a little down on his luck." Vera peered into the car and then turned to Alice and made a funny face. "It appears that he's been living out of his car," she said in a lowered voice, as if someone else might hear.

Alice hesitated, hating to be so nosy, but finally walked over and peeked into the car herself. It was filled with piles of what appeared to be dirty or at least very wrinkled clothes, a sleeping bag, blankets, pillows, lots of fast food containers and miscellaneous pieces of debris. "Goodness," said Alice quietly. "One could only imagine what it must smell like in there."

"Well, as I said, it appears that you have your work cut out for you this week." Vera laughed. "Enjoy your little vacation, Alice."

"Thanks a lot."

"See you tomorrow," called Vera. "If not sooner, and I'll want a complete update."

Alice waved, then went into the house and through to the kitchen.

"Morning, Alice," said Jane as Alice came into the room. "Good walk?"

"Yes," said Alice, noticing Jane's damp hair. "Have you already done your jogging and showered?"

Jane nodded as she cracked an egg into a small mixing bowl. "It was so nice and sunny out that I couldn't resist getting an early start on the day."

"Impressive." Alice peeked into the oven to see what was the source of the delicious aroma that was perfuming the room. "Ah, cinnamon rolls."

"And omelets," said Jane.

"Sounds good."

"I had planned to make waffles," said Jane as she cracked another egg. "But I got to thinking about Laura's diabetes and all that maple syrup."

Alice nodded. "Good for you. Protein is a great way to go. Now, I'm going to run on up and get showered so that I can hurry back down to help you."

Alice tried not to think about Mark as she hurriedly showered and then dressed carefully. Oh, she knew that she was putting more effort than usual into her appearance, especially for a Saturday. Still, she could not help herself. Besides, she knew that if she didn't, Jane would probably give her a lecture.

As she gave her hair a final pat in front of the mirror, she prayed a quick, but heartfelt prayer. *Your will be done, Father. Amen.* Then she went back downstairs.

Chapter  Six

"Don't you look pretty," said Jane as Alice returned to the kitchen.

Alice looked down at her sage green sweater set and olive-colored trousers. "I thought Louise might be glad to see that I'm wearing the set she got me for Christmas. She's mentioned that I hardly ever wear it, but it's just that it's so nice I don't want to spoil it."

"That color is great on you," said Jane as she handed Alice an apron. "Would you please grate this cheese while I run upstairs to get something?"

"Of course."

Alice put on an apron, then hummed to herself as she grated first cheddar cheese, then Monterey jack. She was just finishing up when Jane returned.

"Close your eyes and hold out your hand," said Jane.

"What?"

"Just do it," said Jane.

Alice complied, expecting Jane to put something into her upturned palm, but instead she felt Jane putting something around her wrist.

"Okay, open your eyes."

Alice opened her eyes to see that Jane had clasped a lovely beaded bracelet around her wrist. It had several shades of green beads along with some pretty amber and coral colors.

"That's beautiful, Jane!"

"Thanks. I made it for you for Easter, but when I saw your sweater set, I decided you needed to have it today."

Alice hugged her sister. "The colors are absolutely perfect. I love it."

"Good." Jane grinned. "Now do you want to chop some mushrooms and green onions?"

"Your wish is my command."

Alice had just finished her chopping and was washing the knife and cutting board when someone knocked on the back door. "I'll get it," she called to Jane, who was taking the cinnamon rolls from the oven.

Before she got there, Ethel was letting herself in. "*Yoo-hoo*," she called in her familiar greeting.

"Hey, Aunt Ethel," said Jane as she set the fragrant rolls on the butcher-block countertop. "What's up?"

"I'm all out of coffee," said Ethel as she stood in the doorway with a childish pouting expression. "And I thought maybe I could borrow a bit—"

"Come in, and pour yourself a cup," said Alice as she gave her sister a knowing grin.

Jane winked at Alice. It was their little joke that Ethel always ran out of something if she was hungry, lonely or just wanted to know what was going on at the inn. "Yes, Auntie, do come in," said Jane. "We have plenty of coffee. We have freshly brewed, freshly ground, or even still in the bean form. Take your pick. I suspect you haven't had your breakfast yet."

Ethel's eyebrows lifted hopefully as she leaned over to sniff the cinnamon rolls. "No, as a matter of fact, I haven't."

"Maybe you'd like to join us," said Alice.

Ethel smiled as she helped herself to a cup of coffee. "That sounds perfectly lovely."

"Is Lloyd going to dress up like Mr. Easter Rabbit again this year?" asked Jane.

Acorn Hill's mayor, Lloyd Tynan, was a tireless promoter of town functions and was Ethel's beau.

"Of course, dear," said Ethel sitting down at the kitchen table. "I've already steamed his costume and fluffed his tail."

"Fluffed whose tail?" asked Louise as she came into the kitchen and poured herself a cup of coffee.

"Lloyd's," said Ethel in a matter-of-fact voice.

"I beg your pardon?" Louise turned around and stared at her aunt.

"Mr. Easter Rabbit," explained Ethel.

"Oh," Louise said, looking relieved. "Goodness, one can certainly get confused when hearing only part of a conversation."

"Speaking of conversations," said Jane, "what was going on down here last night, Alice? I heard voices, including yours. Mrs. Winston sounded a bit upset."

Alice explained how Mrs. Winston had thought that Laura had gone missing. She tried not to sound critical of Adam, but Louise was already on that tack.

"That boy," said Louise. "I don't think he is a good influence on Laura. I will be most relieved when Mark arrives and sets things straight."

"Sets things straight?" echoed Jane. "Just how is Mark supposed to do that?"

"Well, if he knows Adam, then he can explain to us his relationship to the young man and he can exert some influence over his behavior."

"You mean teach him some manners?" said Jane in a teasing voice.

"Perhaps."

"I haven't seen him yet," said Ethel, "but I've seen that horrid-looking little car in front of the inn. What an eyesore. Don't you think you could get him to park it in back?"

"I already suggested that to him," said Louise, "but he apparently didn't take me seriously. I'm hoping that Mark will get through to him."

"I wonder why he's so moody," said Jane as she began mixing some cream cheese frosting for the cinnamon rolls. "He's got a great big chip on his shoulder."

Alice went to the dining room to set the table. It was not that she wanted to avoid the conversation about Adam so much as it was that she felt responsible for the young man's behavior. She knew that this was ridiculous, since she had nothing to do with him. He was here because of Mark and, well, Mark was going to be here because of her. *Or was he?* She shook her head at the thought.

"Good morning," said Mr. Winston as he came into the dining room.

Alice smiled. "Good morning." She nodded to a side table where a small selection of newspapers was neatly arranged. "Help yourself to a paper, if you like. I'm sure that breakfast will soon be ready."

"Thank you." He picked up the Philadelphia paper and scanned the headlines.

"Did you sleep well?" she asked.

He nodded as he moved to the table. "Surprisingly well. To be honest, I hadn't expected to be this comfortable in a bed and breakfast."

"Oh, good," she said with one hand on the kitchen door. "Would you like some coffee or tea?"

"Coffee," he said. "I don't know when the rest of my family will be down. My wife was primping in the bathroom and Laura was still asleep."

Alice smiled. "Perhaps that roll-away wasn't too bad after all."

"If you ask me, kids can sleep anywhere. It's only when you get to be old and achy that a good bed becomes imperative."

"True enough," said Alice as she left to get his coffee.

It was not long before the Langleys and Mrs. Winston were also in the dining room. Louise and Ethel joined them, Louise playing the role of hostess and Ethel adding some local spice and flavor to the conversation. Meanwhile Alice helped Jane with the made-to-order omelets.

"Mr. Winston wants cheese and mushrooms," she told Jane. "Mrs. Winston wants mushrooms and onions. The Langleys both want the works. They've already become great fans of the chef."

Jane laughed. "How's Mr. Langley's back?"

"He said it was much better, but I warned him to keep taking the ibuprofen anyway. Too many people stop taking the medicine as soon as they feel better. The next thing you know they're in pain again."

Jane expertly flipped the omelet over, then out of the pan, and Alice carried the plate to the dining room.

"Will your sister mind making an omelet for Laura?" asked Mrs. Winston as Alice set the plate before her. "If she doesn't get up in time, that is. I thought I could take breakfast up to her in a bit—"

"If Laura wants breakfast," her husband interrupted, "she should come down here like the rest of us and get it herself."

"I know, dear," said Mrs. Winston in a low voice, "but you know what happens if she doesn't eat regularly."

"It's no problem," Alice assured them both. "Just let us know how Laura likes her omelet when you're ready to go back—" She stopped in mid-sentence when she saw both Laura and Adam coming into the dining room. "Good morning," she said to them and the others turned to see. Laura had on pale blue sweats and her hair was pulled back into a slightly messy ponytail. Today's sunglasses were square-shaped with tangerine rims. Adam's hair looked even worse than yesterday, and Alice suspected that he had actually slept in his clothes. She wondered if she should offer to let him use their laundry facilities or if that would sound too pushy.

"Laura!" exclaimed Mrs. Winston. "How did you get downstairs—"

"Adam helped me," said Laura in a somewhat irritated voice. "It's no big deal, Mom."

"Come sit down," said Alice as she went over to Laura and guided her to an empty chair next to her mother.

Mrs. Winston gave Alice a grateful smile. "Well, I'm glad you could join us. Jane's omelets are divine."

"And her cinnamon rolls are excellent," said Mr. Winston. "I think I'll have another."

Alice took Laura's and Adam's orders for their omelets and then returned to the kitchen. Before long everyone, except Alice and Jane, had been served.

"Shall we join them?" asked Jane as she slid Alice's omelet onto a plate.

Alice shrugged. "If you want to, but I don't think they'll miss us. It's a full table and Aunt Ethel has been doing a good job of keeping them entertained. She's filling them in on all this week's activities, including a detailed description of Mr. Easter Rabbit's breakfast next Saturday before the big egg hunt."

Jane laughed. "I vote to eat in here."

Soon they were both seated at the kitchen table, and Alice voiced her concerns about Adam spending time with Laura. "I don't know what to do about it," she finally admitted.

"I don't see why you should do anything," said Jane as she peeled off a section of her cinnamon roll. "It's not as if Adam is your personal responsibility, Alice."

"I know . . . it's just that I feel as if it's my fault that he's here and possibly spoiling things for the Winstons."

"I don't see how his help in getting Laura downstairs should be perceived as spoiling anything."

"But you should see their faces, Jane. I can tell they're concerned about his appearance, not to mention his manners. Of course, they're too polite to say anything." Alice lowered her voice although she knew they could not be heard in the dining room. "Honestly, Jane, I am seriously considering telling him that he should do his laundry while he's here. I'm almost certain he slept in his clothes and I think he may have even been living in his car."

Jane laughed. "That's not such a big deal for a kid. I saw a lot of that when I lived in San Francisco."

"It's not exactly the norm for Acorn Hill," said Alice.

"Not exactly."

"Oh, I'll be so relieved when Mark gets here."

"What if?" said Jane in her teasing voice. "What if Mark has never met this kid before? What if he doesn't know him from—from Adam?" Then she started giggling. "What if Mark's real friend is some dignified professor from Harvard and this kid has been sleeping in his bed and—" She burst out laughing now.

Despite herself, Alice laughed too. "Oh dear," she finally muttered. "Wouldn't Louise be furious at me."

"Furious at what?" said Louise as she carried a small stack of dishes into the kitchen.

Alice giggled. "Oh nothing, big sister. I was just being silly."

Louise set the dishes by the sink and then came over to the table. "I am getting quite concerned over your young man," she said in a lowered voice.

Alice nodded. "I know. If it makes you feel any better, I am too."

"But he's not *Alice's* young man," Jane defended.

Louise held one finger in the air. "I say he is. At least until Mark arrives." She looked at Alice now. "I think you should keep tabs on him until then."

"Yes," agreed Alice. "I think you're right."

Jane shrugged as she forked her last bite. "Well, I'll leave all that to you two. As for me, I plan to spend most of my day gardening in this beautiful spring sunshine."

Alice was surprised to see that Adam was still in the dining room when she went to clear the table. He seemed to be trapped in a conversation with Ethel. Alice tried not to appear to be eavesdropping as she slowly gathered up things from the table.

"Do you plan to return to school next year then?" asked Ethel.

He shrugged and looked down at the table. "I don't know."

"But don't you think it would be wise?"

"I don't know."

"My goodness, son!" she exclaimed. "You don't seem to know much, now, do you?"

He stood up and gave her an exasperated look. "I guess not."

"Well, you should work on that," she said. "Folks who don't know much hardly ever amount to much. And I think that—"

"I gotta go," he said, which was more of a good-bye than Alice had heard from him before. Then he hurried out of the dining room.

"Well," said Ethel, clearly insulted. "What a rude young man."

"At least he spoke to you," said Alice as she picked up the last coffee cup. "That's more than I've gotten."

"Really?" Ethel smiled in a coquettish fashion. "Well, I've always had a way with young men."

Alice tried not to giggle as she pushed the door open into the kitchen. Too bad she could not pawn off Adam onto her aunt today. Ethel followed Alice into the kitchen, chattering at her as she went.

"Thank you, girls, for the lovely breakfast," she told them. "I think I'll head off to the store for some coffee. Anything I can pick up for you, Jane?"

"No thanks," said Jane.

"How about you, Alice?" she offered.

"Nothing that I can think of."

"And when is the handsome vet arriving?" asked Ethel.

"I'm not sure," said Alice. "I think it'll be later this afternoon."

"Well, I can't wait to see him," said her aunt as she patted her bright red hair. "And I can't wait to get to the bottom of this Adam mystery."

"You and everyone else," said Alice. Suddenly, even though it was still morning, she felt very, very tired.

"Toodles," Ethel called out as she exited by the back door.

Chapter Seven

"Excuse me," said Alice as she caught Adam coming down the stairs. "I wanted to let you know that you're welcome to use the laundry facilities if you'd like. I can show you how everything works—"

"I don't want to do laundry," he told her in a voice that seemed to be saying "butt out."

"But I've noticed that . . ." Alice paused. "Well, perhaps you'd like me to do some laundry for you. I don't mind."

He studied her for a moment. "Look, you're probably just trying to be nice, but I don't need it, okay? I'm not going to be here for long, so maybe you should just pretend like I'm not here at all."

"But I—"

"Just chill," he said in an irritated tone.

She nodded as she watched him heading toward the front door. Then, remembering Louise's warning, she decided to persist. "Adam," she said in her most authoritative voice.

He turned and looked at her.

"My sister would appreciate it if you parked your car in the parking area reserved for the inn. We try to keep the street clear of vehicles." She cleared her throat. "City ordinances, you know."

He rolled his eyes. "Yeah, whatever."

"And," she continued, "are you going out?"

He exhaled loudly, shoved his hands into his pockets, but did not answer.

"I just wondered," she said. "In case Mark arrives and you're not here. When shall I tell him that you'll be back?"

"I'm not gonna be gone long," he said, reaching for the doorknob.

Just then the door opened and Mrs. Winston and Laura came in. "Oh, hello," said Mrs. Winston when she nearly ran into Adam. "We just took a little walk around town."

"Hey," he said, looking at Laura.

"Adam?" asked Laura eagerly.

"Yeah," he answered. "I'm just heading out."

"Where are you going?" she asked.

"Just to town, you know."

"Need any company?" she asked.

Alice noticed the look of alarm in Mrs. Winston's eyes. "Uh, Laura," she said quickly. "You told me you were tired and we just went—"

"Not as much tired as bored," said Laura.

"You can come if you want," said Adam.

"Oh, I don't know," began Mrs. Winston.

"It's just to town, Mom," said Laura. "It's not like he's going to kidnap me or anything." She almost smiled now and Alice realized how pretty she would be if she smiled more. "Are you, Adam?"

He shook his head, then remembering that she couldn't see him, quickly said, "Nah, I wasn't planning on it."

"Great," said Laura as she reached out for him.

"Uh, okay," he said as he took her hand.

"But, I'm not sure that it's—"

"Both you and Dad keep telling me to get out and do

something," Laura said as Adam guided her out the still-open door.

"But when will you be back?" implored her worried mother.

Laura shrugged, but continued going.

"Adam said he wouldn't be gone long," offered Alice, certain that she felt as concerned as Mrs. Winston did. "After all, Acorn Hill's not a very big town."

"Yes, I realize that." Mrs. Winston stood looking out the door as Adam and Laura walked over to his car. "Oh dear," said Mrs. Winston. "I didn't know they would be driving."

Alice went over to see. Laura was waiting on the sidewalk as Adam opened a rear door to his car, then dug around as if looking for something. Finally, he emerged with a gray sweatshirt that he pulled over his head. "Oh," said Alice in relief. "Maybe he's not going to drive after all."

To her dismay, he then opened the front passenger door, threw some things in the back and helped Laura get in.

"Oh no," said Mrs. Winston.

Alice watched helplessly as Adam then stooped over and helped Laura find the seatbelt. "At least he's being safe," she offered.

Mrs. Winston just nodded, but her expression was one of complete hopelessness.

"I'm sure they'll be just fine." The truth was, Alice was not so sure. She did not trust Adam any farther than she could throw him. Oh, if only Mark would get here. Soon!

Alice tried to look busy during the next hour, puttering about but really accomplishing little more than keeping a wary eye on the street in front of the inn, hoping and even praying that the two young guests would return soon.

Finally, she heard voices coming in the back door and hurried toward the kitchen to see Adam and Laura being led in by Jane. "Feel free to help yourself if you want a snack," Jane said, as she removed her gardening gloves and stuffed them into a pocket of her overalls. "There's fresh fruit and some oatmeal cookies."

"I'm cool," said Adam.

"Do you have any apples?" asked Laura.

As Jane was getting Laura an apple, Adam walked past Alice without saying a word in response to her greeting.

"Did you have a good time?" asked Alice.

"It was okay," said Laura. She took a bite of the apple. "Adam?" she said, unaware that he had left the room.

"He's gone," said Alice.

"Oh." Now Laura looked troubled.

"Do you want me to help you find your mom?" offered Alice.

"Yeah, I guess."

Alice took Laura's arm and led her through the inn. "I didn't see Adam's car," she said as they came to the staircase.

"He said you told him to park it off the street," said Laura.

"Oh yes," said Alice. "That's right."

"Laura!" exclaimed Mrs. Winston as she came down the hallway that led to the library. "You're back."

"I told you I'd be back," said Laura in a flat voice.

"Good," said Mr. Winston from behind his wife. "I want to take my favorite ladies out for a little ride and then some lunch." He held up a map and travel brochure. "I've discovered some places of local interest that I think we should investigate."

Laura sighed. "Not me, Dad, I'm tired. I think I'll just rest."

"But what about—"

She cut him off. "Seriously, Dad. I just want to listen to my new CD and maybe take a nap. You and Mom go on ahead. I'll be fine."

"Oh, I don't think—"

"Laura's right," Mr. Winston said to his wife. "I think you and I should go ahead as planned. And Laura can rest. Then maybe we can all do something together this afternoon. Is that agreeable to you, Laura?"

She shrugged. "Yeah, whatever."

"But will you be okay by yourself, honey?" asked her mother.

"I'll be here all day," said Alice. "If Laura needs any—"

"I'll be fine," said Laura. "I'll just stay in the room and rest. Okay?"

"Well . . ." her mother did not look convinced.

"She'll be fine," said Mr. Winston as he took his wife's arm and led her to the front door.

"Have a good time," said Alice. She turned to Laura. "Do you want me to help you to your room now?"

"Yeah, I guess so."

After Laura was safely in her room, Alice went upstairs to get her new mystery. She had decided that she would stay nearby, at least within shouting distance, just in case Laura needed something. She settled herself in the parlor, choosing an upright chair that was close to the door, as she attempted to focus her mind on the sentences before her. Some time passed, and she glanced at her watch and was surprised to see that it was almost noon. She knew that Laura's diabetes and medication made it important for her to eat at regular intervals, so she decided to go and check on the girl. By the time she reached the second floor, Laura and Adam were on the landing discussing the possibility of going out to lunch.

"My treat," insisted Laura.

Adam shrugged. "Yeah, like, whatever."

"Are you going out again?" asked Alice.

"We're going to get some lunch in town," said Laura.

"Oh." Then, thinking that she might head this off, she said, "But there's plenty to eat here and Jane said to—"

"I thought this was a bed and *breakfast*," said Laura.

"Well, it is—"

"We already had breakfast." She reached out for Adam and he took her hand. "So we want to go out and get some lunch."

Alice had nothing else to say that she thought would dissuade these two young people. She watched as they slowly headed downstairs, praying that Laura would be safe in Adam's care.

Finally, they were gone and Alice went into the kitchen. She was not actually hungry. Mostly she was nervous and hoped that perhaps Jane would be taking a lunch break.

"Hey, you," said Jane when Alice came in. "I just saw the odd couple leaving."

Despite her worries, Alice had to laugh. "That just about describes them, doesn't it?"

"I think so. I mean, here we have Laura, a cute little preppy that any parent would be proud of—well, other than her attitude, which is excusable under the circumstances—and then you have Adam, the kid who looks like he's been living on the streets or maybe rooming with Oscar the Grouch."

"Oscar the Grouch? Do you mean the one who played the slob in *The Odd Couple*?"

Jane laughed. "No, I mean Oscar the Grouch, the puppet who lives in a trash can. Didn't you ever watch *Sesame Street*?"

"Oh, I've seen bits of it on the children's ward at the hospital."

Jane took out a loaf of bread. "I used to watch it with kids when I was babysitting. Oscar the Grouch was always messy and grumbling. Adam reminds me of him a little."

Alice chuckled. "Well, let's keep that to ourselves."

"I'm making a grilled cheese sandwich," said Jane. "Want one?"

"Yes, please." Alice went to the refrigerator for the cheese and pickles. "I offered to do Adam's laundry," she told Jane as she set the items on the counter.

"And he didn't take you up on it?" She picked up a knife. "That kid's not only rude, but dumb too."

"Too bad," said Alice as she got plates. "Where's Louise?"

"She walked to town. Meeting Viola for lunch."

"Oh, good," said Alice. "Maybe she'll see Adam and Laura and keep an eye on them. Or call me if it looks like anything is amiss."

"If Louise sees Adam out with Laura, she'll probably call the police."

"Oh, I don't think . . ."

Jane laughed. "She'll probably assume that he's abducted her and planning on holding her hostage or something."

Alice sighed. "Okay, in that case, let's hope that Louise does not see them at lunch." She shook her head. "I feel so bad about all this."

"Just remember," said Jane. "No matter what happens, it's *not* your fault. Neither of those kids is your responsibility."

"So you say . . ."

After lunch, Alice resumed her post. She knew that Jane was right, that these kids were not her responsibility, but she could not help feeling concern for Laura, and more than anything she wished that Adam had never shown up at their inn. It was clear that he did not want to be here and was only here to see Mark. Or so she assumed. What a relief it would be to find out that Mark did not even know Adam and that this was all simply a silly mistake. They would kindly send Adam on his way to who knew where and then they could all get on with life.

Chapter  Eight

It was nearly three when Adam and Laura returned. Alice was a nervous wreck. It probably didn't help the state of her mind that she was reading a mystery that involved an abducted woman. Maybe Louise was correct about her taste in books. She set the novel aside and rose to greet them.

"Did you have a nice lunch?" she asked.

"Yeah," said Laura. "Considering the size of this town, I suppose it was okay."

"I'm going to my room," said Adam, and without offering to take Laura upstairs, he disappeared.

Laura looked somewhat dismayed and, once again, Alice felt sorry for her. "What would you like to do?" asked Alice.

Laura shrugged. "I'm kind of tired."

"Want me to help you to your room?"

"Yeah, please."

With Laura safely in her room, Alice resisted the urge to barricade the door and went upstairs to her own room. There she attempted to work on the baby quilt, leaving her door open and trying to keep her ears tuned in case Laura needed something or attempted to make another foray from her room. Alice could not stop her, of course, but at least she would know where Laura was if the Winstons came home and wondered where their daughter had wandered off to. Alice sincerely hoped that they would get home before Laura and Adam decided on some new excursion.

Alice had been relieved to see that the Langleys had decided to walk to town this afternoon. She had told them about the Coffee Shop's delicious blackberry pie and had assured Mr. Langley that the walk to town was a mild form of exercise that would probably be therapeutic for his back. And now, she told herself, she should enjoy this peaceful time during which it seemed that nothing much was going on at the inn. She considered taking a nap herself so that she would be refreshed and energetic by the time Mark arrived. She felt a current of nervous energy running through her, however, and suspected that even if she were to lie down, she would not be able to sleep. And so, she carefully pinned and then checked each quilt piece to be sure the right side was up, then meticulously sewed, pausing now and then to listen to the silence of the inn.

Concentrating on her sewing diverted her thoughts from Mark, and she was surprised when she looked up at the clock to discover it was nearly five. Concerned about Laura, Alice went down to the second floor to look around. All was quiet, but this did not reassure her. Deciding that she could use Laura's health and her need to have regular snacks to balance out her insulin shots to excuse the interruption, Alice knocked on Laura's door. When no one answered, Alice grew even more concerned. *What if Laura has had a seizure?* She hated to intrude, but she felt that she had to check on the girl. Alice quietly opened the door and glanced around the room? "Laura?" she called. No answer. Alice tiptoed over to the open bathroom door, but she saw that the room was empty.

She stood in the middle of the room gathering her thoughts, then she decided to check on Adam. She didn't care if he was insulted by her doing so. She knocked on his door and when he didn't answer she took the liberty of peeking into his room. To her surprise, it was completely devoid of any personal items, as if he had checked out. Alice closed the door and headed downstairs. Maybe her sisters would know what was up.

Jane was putting away her gardening tools when Alice came out into the backyard and asked her about Laura and Adam.

"I haven't seen them," said Jane. "But Adam's car isn't in the parking area and it's not out front."

"Oh dear." Alice held the shed door open for Jane. "I don't suppose you've seen the Winstons?"

"Sorry. But I've been back here all afternoon." Jane hung up her hoe and closed the door. "I did see the Langleys coming back from their walk. They said they were going to have a little nap and then perhaps try going out for dinner if Mr. Langley's back continued to hold up."

Alice nodded. "Oh, good for them."

"Don't worry about Laura," said Jane. "She's seventeen and responsible for herself. And keep in mind even her parents can't seem to control her. Who knows, maybe this is a good thing for her. After all, her parents have been concerned about her lack of independence."

"That's true. It's funny, isn't it? Sometimes you want something so badly, and then you get it and you're not sure that you want it anymore."

Jane looked at her sister, her eyebrows arching slightly. "Are we still talking about Laura?"

Alice gave a rueful little laugh. "I don't know. Anything I can do to help in the kitchen while you're cleaning up?" She pulled a twig out of Jane's hair.

Jane looked at her overalls and held up her dirty hands. "You really think I need to clean up?"

Alice smiled. "Not if you're trying to impress Adam."

"Yeah, right. If you could go ahead and start a green salad that would be great. Do you think Mark will be here in time for dinner?"

"I have no idea. It was Louise who took his reservation."

"Well, I put a roast in the oven, just in case. Although he may want to take you out tonight, Alice."

"I doubt it," said Alice. "Remember we still have the Adam factor."

"That's true. So does that mean you don't think he ran off with Laura?"

"Well, let's hope not permanently."

As Alice shredded lettuce and peeled carrots and cucumbers, she wondered where Laura's parents were and how they would react if they came home to discover that Laura and Adam were gone and that no one knew where they went. Once again, she prayed. This time she prayed primarily for Laura. Alice could not imagine how it would feel to be blind. She knew that God could bring good out of what seemed like a terrible situation, but Alice could not imagine what good thing that might be. Under the surface of her worry for Laura was annoyance with Adam. She had specifically told him that he should not take Laura anywhere without her parents' permission. He could have at least informed Alice that they were going out.

"Hello in there?" called a familiar male voice.

Alice dropped the vegetable peeler and listened.

"Mark!" she heard Louise say. Alice attempted to compose herself, but already her heart was beating so hard that she felt like she had just run a footrace.

"I am so glad to see you," said Louise. Hearing her, Alice

felt that the primary reason her sister was glad had to do with Adam. "Alice?" Louise called out. "Are you down here?"

"I'm in the kitchen," she called back as she hurriedly took off her apron and rinsed her hands. "I'll be out in a minute." Before she finished drying her hands, however, Louise had brought Mark in.

"Look who's here," said Louise, proudly showing off Mark as if she had produced him herself.

Alice smiled and extended her hand. "Oh, it's so good to see you again." She examined him more closely. "You look wonderful—a little thinner perhaps, and there's a bit more white in your beard. Very distinguished."

He looked into her eyes as he continued to hold her hand in a warm grasp. "You look even more lovely than the last time I saw you," he finally proclaimed.

"Oh, Mark . . ."

"As does your sister and this inn and the entire charming town of Acorn Hill." He released her hand and turned to Louise with a smile. "Am I just getting old or is life getting sweeter?"

She laughed. "Well, since you're asking me, I must admit that age does sweeten a few things."

"Mark!" cried Jane as she entered the room. "You're finally here."

"In the flesh," he said. "And as I was telling your sisters, everything about this town looks lovelier than the last time I saw it. As do you, Jane."

"Thank you, kind sir." She laughed. "We need more charming gentlemen around here."

"Speaking of gentlemen," said Mark, turning back to Alice, "has my guest arrived yet?"

The sisters exchanged a quick look, then Alice asked,

"Adam?" holding on to the hope that Adam had nothing to do with Mark.

He smiled. "Oh, good, he's here. Kids sometimes have different ideas about schedules."

"Yes," said Alice. "He actually arrived yesterday." She thought, *Was it really only a day ago that he came? Goodness, so much has happened.*

"Is he in his room?" asked Mark.

"Well, to be honest, I'm not sure where he is," she admitted with a frown.

He noticed Alice's expression and asked, "Is something wrong?"

Alice glanced uneasily at her sisters, unsure of how best to proceed. "Perhaps we should talk," she said to him.

"Maybe we could take a walk," he suggested. "I'd like to stretch my legs after that drive."

"That's an excellent idea."

Soon they were outside and Mark was admiring Jane's handiwork in the garden. "I'm not exaggerating, Alice. Everything looks so lovely to me in this town. Maybe it's the springtime or maybe I'm just glad to be here."

"It's a lovely time of year."

He looked at her. "Or maybe it's you."

She felt herself blushing. Unprepared to be moving in this direction so quickly, she decided it was best simply to express her concerns about Adam openly. "Mark, we need to talk about Adam," she said in a serious voice.

"Certainly." He nodded as they continued to walk. "I didn't realize he'd get here before me or I would've explained his situation. I'm sorry."

"His situation?"

"Yes, he's going through a rough time and I feel it's my

responsibility to help see him through. I thought if he met me here in Acorn Hill, we could discuss his future."

She cleared her throat. "Uh, what exactly is your relationship to Adam?"

"Didn't I tell you?"

"No, not that I recall."

Mark slapped his forehead. "I'm getting forgetful in my old age."

Alice felt as if she was holding her breath now, waiting for Mark to answer.

"Adam is my godson," he said as they neared the house where Vera and her husband, Fred, lived. "His father Gregory Peterson was my best friend from grammar school and throughout college. He was the best."

"Was?"

Mark nodded sadly. "Evidently, I didn't tell you about this either. I suspect it was because I was so depressed by the news myself, I probably didn't want to burden you with it."

"What happened?"

"Gregory and his wife Amy were killed in a car wreck."

"Oh dear, how tragic."

"Adam had just started his second year of college. An only child, he was shattered by the loss."

"Of course." Now Alice felt bad for not having been kinder to the boy.

"His grandmother, who is quite elderly, wrote me that Adam was having some problems and that she was concerned. Apparently, he has dropped out of college to travel, he told her. She thought that he was just going through a phase, grieving, or something."

"That is entirely possible."

"Yes, but months passed and he continued living in what

she describes as his 'dead-end' lifestyle. She was very frustrated and hoped that I could help. That's why I invited him to meet me here."

"I see."

He paused and gave her a concerned look. "I hope it hasn't been an inconvenience."

Alice decided simply to tell him what had been going on and how it had been disturbing to her and her sisters. Even as she related those things, she felt guilty for the pettiness of their assumptions. "I feel so bad now," she admitted. "I mean, if I'd known what Adam was going through, well, I'm sure I would've been more patient, as would have Louise and Jane. But we just weren't aware. And then there is the situation with Laura and her parents. The Winstons are so worried about her blindness and how she's adjusting and, well, Adam has just seemed to exacerbate things. And now with them both missing—"

"Missing?" Mark sounded alarmed now. "What do you mean?"

She held up her hands. "I'm not sure what I mean. All I know is that they're both gone. And judging by Adam's room, he could be gone for good."

"Oh, I don't think—"

"No, Mark. I'm sorry. I shouldn't have said that. I have no reason to think such a thing. I guess it's just that I've been worried . . ."

"No, I'm the one to apologize. I'm so sorry that having Adam here has been troubling to you." He sighed deeply.

"Well, I feel better about everything now. But to be honest, I am worried about him, Mark. After what you've told me I would guess that he is depressed. That would certainly explain his lack of care about his personal hygiene and—"

"His personal hygiene?"

"You'll understand what I mean when you see him. He's been living in his car. Well, it all makes sense now. When I offered to do his laundry, he said no, but of course, if he's depressed, he probably really doesn't care." She realized that she was almost talking to herself. "I'm sorry to go on and on."

"No, it's good to know these things. It helps me to evaluate the situation before I speak to him. I haven't been around him that much since he grew up. I used to see him a lot when he was a little kid and his parents still lived in Philadelphia. We had some great times together and I thought he was the greatest. I used to take him on small veterinary assignments with me and he was actually quite helpful with the animals. Then the family moved a few hours away and my practice grew increasingly busy, and I rarely saw them after that. To be honest, those few times I did see the teenaged Adam, I thought that he had become selfish and spoiled. He never seemed to treat his parents with much respect, and I guess I didn't really enjoy being around him."

"Mark!" Alice pointed to the car coming down the street. "That's him! That's Adam's car."

They both waved from where they were standing on the opposite side of the street, but Adam did not appear to notice.

"Oh dear," said Alice, clapping her hand over her mouth.

"What?"

"He's alone! Where is Laura?"

They both turned around and quickly began walking back toward the inn. "Trust me," said Mark, "we'll soon find out."

Chapter  Nine

They were both slightly out of breath when they finally reached the inn. They discovered Adam near his car, which to Alice's dismay was parked once again on the street in front of the inn. Adam was standing slightly hunched, lighting a cigarette.

"Adam!" called Mark as they hurried over.

Adam looked up from his lighter. "Hey," he said in a casual voice, as if he saw Mark every day. He snapped his lighter closed, dropped it into one of the pockets on his baggy pants and took a long drag from his cigarette.

For a moment it looked as if Mark were going to hug Adam, but the young man shifted away and so Mark shook his hand while lightly patting him on the back.

"You smoke now?" said Mark in a surprisingly parental tone.

Adam shrugged and slowly exhaled the smoke from his nostrils as he studied Mark and Alice.

"I suppose you've heard all the lectures about how that stuff can kill you?"

Adam shrugged again, then took another drag. "We're all going to die anyway, Mark. That's the unavoidable human condition."

Mark frowned but said nothing.

"I'm wondering about Laura," began Alice, "I—uh—I thought maybe she was with you."

"Well, you can see that she's not."

"Do you know where she is?" asked Mark.

Adam shrugged. "Why should I know?"

"Haven't you been with her?" asked Mark. "Alice said that you—"

"What?" snapped Adam. "That I abducted her?"

"No, not at all," said Alice. "I only said that you two had been spending time together. Laura is not at the inn, and I don't know where she has gone. And, well, her mother had asked me to keep an eye on her. I'm just worried."

"Understandable," said Mark, patting Alice on the back. "A missing blind girl is a serious problem."

Hearing it put like that only proved to be more upsetting to Alice. She felt her eyes tearing and she reached in her trouser pocket for a tissue. "Oh dear," she said.

"So, are you saying that you don't know where she is?" Mark asked Adam again, this time in a very firm voice.

"Man, what is it with you people?" snapped Adam as he dropped his cigarette and snuffed it out beneath his grimy tennis shoe. "Say Adam, how are you doing? How's life treating you, Adam? Just questions and accusations like you actually think I did something to Laura. It figures!" He shook his head and walked around to the other side of his car, climbed in, started the engine, gunned it and took off.

"Oh dear," said Alice. "He is upset."

"I didn't handle that well," admitted Mark as he rubbed his beard.

"I'm afraid that's my fault," said Alice. "I shouldn't have dumped all that information on you before you'd had a chance to speak to Adam."

"Your concern for the girl was legitimate." He sighed. "I wonder if this is how it would feel to be parents."

"Oh dear," said Alice. "In that case, we should be thankful that we're not."

Mark laughed. "Well, I'm sure that Adam will cool off. If not, I may go out to look for him and see if we can iron this thing out. I have to admit that I don't much care for his attitude, and you're right about his appearance."

"Don't forget that he's probably depressed," Alice reminded him. "That could explain everything."

"I know that's true, but you just have to deal with grief and keep on keeping on."

"Maybe that works for some people," said Alice, "but it's not like that for everyone. Some people need professional help."

Just then she noticed another familiar car approaching the inn. "*Oh no!*"

"Who is it?"

"Laura's parents," gasped Alice. "Oh dear, what on earth am I going to tell them?"

As the car drew closer, Alice felt her knees growing weaker. "This is so awful, Mark." She stared down at the ground, almost afraid to even see the Winstons face to face. *Oh, what will I say?* she thought.

"Don't worry," he said. "I'm here with you. Somehow we'll—" he paused. "Say, do they have two daughters, Alice?"

"No." She looked up in time to see Mrs. Winston happily waving from the front seat and Laura, glum as usual, sitting in the back. "That's her," said Alice. "That's Laura!"

Mark smiled. "So, all's well that ends well."

"What about Adam?" she asked in a meek voice, wondering which was worse, a missing blind girl or a brokenhearted, depressed boy. *God help me*, she prayed silently as they walked back to the house. *And help Adam too.*

Louise showed Mark to his room while Alice returned to the kitchen to help Jane. While they worked, she told Jane the whole story about Adam and finally how she and Mark had practically accused him of kidnapping Laura. "I feel so bad about it," she confessed. "Adam must despise me."

"Sounds like that kid needs some help," said Jane as she seasoned the gravy.

"That's what I told Mark." Alice unwrapped a stick of butter and set it in the butter dish. "Even so, I wish I had handled the Laura situation better." She shook her head. "I don't know how the Winstons came in and got Laura and left the inn without my hearing."

"Well, you said that you were sewing. It's possible they came while your machine was running."

"I suppose."

"With both the Langleys and the Winstons going out for dinner tonight, we could eat in the dining room," said Jane.

"Do you want me to set it up in there?"

"It's up to you, Alice." Jane checked on the oven. "Oh, by the way, I got conned into inviting Aunt Ethel for dinner tonight."

Alice sighed. "Why does that not surprise me?"

"Yes, she can't wait to get her hands on your 'young man' as she calls Mark. She wants to hear all about his veterinary adventures."

"How did she persuade you?"

"She has the most beautiful daylilies in her side yard, and I've been begging her to share some with me. They're an old-fashioned variety that's hard to find. So this afternoon she traipsed over and announced that she was just dividing the clump and asked if I would like some. Well, I jumped up from planting onions and ran over to her house and while I was putting my lilies into a box she mentioned how she hoped she'd get to see Mark when he arrived and was I planning some special dinner?"

"So she bribed you with daylilies."

"Basically."

"Leave it to Aunt Ethel."

"At least she's bringing dessert."

"Let me guess," said Alice.

"Peach tarts," they said simultaneously.

"Mark will be pleased," said Alice. "He loves Auntie's tarts."

It was not long before they were all seated around the dining room table. "Isn't this nice?" said Mark as he looked at the women surrounding him. He offered to say the blessing. "For dear friends and good food and fine fellowship, dear Lord, we give You thanks. Amen."

Alice looked up and glanced at the one empty place. "I wish Adam could've joined us."

"No luck in your search for him?" said Jane as she passed the rolls.

"I scoured the town," said Mark as he ladled some gravy onto his meat. "If he was in Acorn Hill, I'm sure I would've found him."

"Do you think he went home?" asked Louise.

Alice glanced uncomfortably at Mark. Louise and Ethel had yet to hear all the details about their young guest. Perhaps they didn't need to. Certainly, it wasn't Alice's place to inform them. Not, at least, while Mark was here.

"As far as I know," began Mark, "Adam has been living in his car." Then he went on to explain about the death of Adam's parents and his grandmother's recent worries. "His parents left insurance money for him, but it's tied up in a trust fund controlled by the grandmother. She told me that the money is only to be used for college and living expenses until he's twenty-five, but when Adam dropped out of college, she froze all funds. And now Adam is on his own."

"Oh, what a terrible thing, losing his parents and so suddenly," said Louise. "The poor boy must be suffering."

"My parents died when I was young," said Ethel. "If it hadn't been for my brother, these girls' dear father, well, I don't know what would've become of me. He and his sweet wife took me right into their home. Do you girls remember that?" she asked. "I mean Alice and Louise. Of course, Jane hadn't been born yet."

Louise and Alice nodded. Ethel took a bite of her Yorkshire pudding, then continued. "I did what I could to help with the girls. And then after Madeleine died, well, I was glad to be there to help Daniel and his three motherless girls through their time of need."

"You really do need family at a time like that," said Alice. "Unfortunately for Adam, he only has his grandmother for family. Amy's only sister died quite young from leukemia and Gregory was an only child."

"It is good that he has you," said Louise.

"That's right," said Ethel. "His parents were wise to pick such a responsible person for their son's godfather."

Mark laughed. "I'm not so sure about that. At the time, even though I was in my forties, I would not have described myself as anything that resembled responsible. But Gregory and I had always been good friends. We'd been as close as brothers growing up. Been rowdy college boys together. I had even been the best man at their wedding about ten years before Adam was born."

"Wow," said Jane, "that was a long wait for a baby."

"Yes," said Mark, "there was some problem about getting pregnant, and they were ecstatic when Adam came along. I still remember the christening. You never saw prouder parents. But honestly, I think their choice of me as godfather had more to do with friendship than anything else. I certainly had no experience with kids. To be perfectly honest, I didn't even know what the role of a godparent was. I'm not sure that I do now. Oh, I went to Adam's christening, and I always send him gifts for birthdays, Christmas, special occasions. But other than that? I'm really not sure."

"Well, when Father did baptisms," began Alice, "he would always point out that godparents were to be responsible for a child's spiritual upbringing should a parent be unable to perform that duty."

Mark's eyes grew wide. "Seriously?"

"My father took it very seriously," said Alice. "He would question the godparent to discern if they were really willing to commit to this important role. He would remind them that, while it was an honor to be chosen for a godparent, it was also a big responsibility that should last a lifetime."

Mark nodded. "That's a big commitment."

"Well," said Ethel in a time-to-change-the-subject tone, "did I tell you girls about Lloyd's latest idea to have a barbecue this year?" She launched into a long-winded story about how Lloyd Tynan had met this Southern gentleman at a mayor's conference, and the man had the most wonderful recipe for ribs. "And Lloyd has invited him up here so that he can teach Lloyd how to make it, and then Lloyd is going to put on a barbecue that not one of his guests will ever forget."

Jane and Alice had just begun clearing the table when Adam walked in. Alice went over to him. "Oh, Adam," she said, "we're so glad you made it." She pointed to the unused place setting. "There's still lots of roast beef and I can reheat the gravy and the Yorkshire pudding and—"

"You don't have to be nice to me just because Mark is here."

Alice felt her eyes growing large. "Well, that's not it. I just feel very sorry for the way I assumed that Laura would be with you. I hope that you'll forgive me."

"So she showed up?"

Alice thought she saw the slightest flicker of interest in his eyes. As small as it was, it gave her hope. "Yes. It turned out that she'd been with her parents."

"Come and join us," said Mark. "Jane is an excellent cook."

"Yes," said Ethel and she launched into a history of Jane's culinary achievements as a chef in San Francisco.

Jane chuckled as she turned on the stove to reheat the gravy. "Aunt Ethel's tales get better with every telling, don't they? To hear her talk, you'd think that Wolfgang Puck would be knocking down my door."

"Next thing we know, you'll be a featured chef on a cooking show." Alice turned away from Jane as she put the pudding into the microwave to warm. She did not want to admit it, but Adam's comment that she was being nice because of Mark still stung.

Jane chuckled. The microwave dinged and Alice got a potholder to remove the dish.

"He's getting to you, isn't he?" said Jane as she refilled the gravy boat with hot gravy.

"Who?"

"Adam." Jane came over to Alice. "He may have lost his parents, Alice, but that doesn't mean he had to lose his manners too. I wouldn't let him talk to me like that."

"But I couldn't . . ."

"I realize that you and Mark have some things to figure out," she continued, "and while it's none of my business, you better figure out this thing with Adam too. A kid like that could drive a real wedge into any relationship."

Alice did not respond since they were already heading back into the dining room with the reheated food. Now Mark was regaling everyone with an exciting story about piranhas and how an Amazon River guide had lost some fingers to the feisty fish. Alice felt relieved that Adam seemed mildly interested in the graphic tale, but she noticed the chilly look he gave her when she set the warmed Yorkshire pudding before him.

She told herself that Adam was still irked about her assumption that he had something to do with Laura's disappearance. And she could not blame him. Even so, she felt it might be deeper than that. She wondered if he resented her relationship with Mark. Perhaps he felt that this was a time when he needed someone like Mark in his life, but then there was Alice just getting in the way.

Chapter  Ten

"Shall we have dessert in the living room?" suggested Louise. "Then perhaps Mark would show us some of his photos of his recent trip."

"Don't twist my arm," teased Mark.

"That's an excellent idea," said Alice as she picked up a serving dish. "Why don't all of you head on in there while I take care of these—"

"Nothing doing." Jane grabbed the dish from Alice. "I've got everything under control."

"And I can help Jane," said Ethel as she picked up Mark's dinner plate and headed toward the kitchen.

Alice knew her sister would not be pleased by this offer, since Ethel had a tendency to talk more than help, but Jane simply smiled and continued to clear the table. Alice suspected that her loquacious aunt would rather be in the center of the limelight than share it with something as mundane as travel photos.

They began working their way through the photos, which Mark had nicely arranged in albums with notations explaining them. Alice was pleased to see that Adam actually seemed to be interested. He even asked Mark several rather intelligent questions that began to give her hope for this young man.

"If you ever give up veterinary work," said Alice as she studied a particularly lovely shot of a sunset on a river, "you could consider photography, Mark. Some of these are worthy of framing."

"Well, thank you," said Mark. "I was afraid that I took too many photos. But I figured I might never get back there again."

"Why not?" asked Adam.

Mark smiled. "I guess because I'm getting old."

"Aren't you about the same age as my dad was?"

"That's right."

"Well, that's not that old. Old is my grandma's age. She's like ninety, I think."

"Yes," said Mark. "I'm not as old as your grandmother, though sometimes I feel like it."

"Here comes dessert," sang out Ethel as she and Jane came in bearing trays laden with small peach tarts buried under miniature mountains of whipped cream.

"I hope everyone wanted whipped cream," said Jane, "since Aunt Ethel got a bit carried away."

Ethel laughed. "Well, Jane has all the best toys in her kitchen. Her fancy whipped cream maker was so much fun that I just couldn't stop myself."

After everyone had been served, Ethel sat next to Mark and told him in explicit detail about her latest ailment, a bad bunion on her left foot. Apparently, she thought an animal doctor should know about human medicine as well. The others brought Jane up to date on the photos, and Adam even explained a few things to her.

"Wow, Adam," she said. "You seem to know a lot about faraway places. Have you traveled a lot?"

"No. But I've read a lot about travel and I used to think I'd like to go around the world."

"Used to?" asked Jane.

He shrugged and looked down at his empty dessert plate. "Yeah, back when I was a little kid."

"But don't you still think it would be exciting as a grownup?" she asked.

He seemed to consider this. "Maybe."

"Maybe if you finished college," suggested Alice, "then perhaps you could get a job that—"

"Look," Adam pointed his finger at Alice and the room grew suddenly quiet, "I don't need you telling me what to do, okay?"

Alice actually started, then nodded. "That's fine." She quickly stood and busily gathered several empty plates as if that was just what she had intended to do. Then she headed for the door, but not soon enough to miss Mark's attempt at correcting his discourteous godson.

"That's not a very respectful way to speak to an elder," he began in a quiet voice.

Fortunately, she was down the hall before Adam could respond. One thing was clear to her, painfully clear: Adam disliked her. She knew it was not her imagination. Furthermore, despite her good intentions, she did not like him. Perhaps that was the most disturbing discovery of the evening.

She heard someone behind her and, worried Mark might be coming to apologize for Adam's impolite behavior, she hastened her step. She did not want him to see her like this, not with these hot tears running down her flushed cheeks, but her hands were full and all she could do was hurry to the kitchen and hope to dry her face on a tissue before he noticed.

She was relieved to discover it was Jane who had followed.

"Oh, Alice," Jane said when she saw the tears. She set aside Alice's stack of plates and gave her sister a big hug.

"I feel so silly," muttered Alice as they stepped apart.

"That Adam," Jane shook her head. "He was just making

me start to like him and then he goes and says something as dimwitted as that."

"Oh, he's just unhappy," said Alice as she reached for a tissue to dry her tears.

"And he wants you to be unhappy with him? Misery loves company?"

Alice shrugged. "I think he may resent me."

"Of course he does," said Jane. "He probably sees Mark as someone who was going to rescue him and you as someone who might mess things up."

Alice nodded. "Yes, that's what I was thinking too."

"Just be patient with him."

"I'm trying."

Jane gently rubbed Alice's back. "I know you are, sweetie. You're doing far better than I would be under the same circumstances."

Jane's sympathy only made Alice cry harder. "Goodness," she said as she used another tissue to dry her eyes, "I don't know what's wrong with me tonight. I feel as if I'm falling apart."

"I know what's wrong," said Jane. "And I'm going to give you the same remedy that you once gave me."

Alice soon found herself excused from the evening's gathering. Before she could protest, Jane had escorted her up the back stairway to her room where the door was quickly closed to shut out the sounds of piano music coming from down below.

"Don't worry about a single thing," promised Jane as she filled Alice's tub with hot, lavender-scented water. "I will tell everyone that you've come down with a migraine or perhaps something even more exotic. What was that disease that Mark was telling us about?"

"Oh no!" Alice certainly hoped that Jane would not lie on

her behalf. Then she touched her forehead. "Actually, my head is throbbing a bit."

"See," said Jane as she lit a scented candle, then reached into her pocket to produce several homemade truffles, which she artistically arranged along the side of the tub. "Take these and call me in the morning."

Despite her misery, Alice laughed. "You're an angel."

"Hey, I learned from the best." She handed Alice her bathrobe. "Now, I want you to just relax and totally empty your head. Hey, do you have a good book?"

Soon Alice was steeping in bubbles, munching on chocolates and slowly erasing the day's worries as she got lost in her mystery. When she finally climbed into bed, she realized that sometimes the best way to deal with a bad situation was simply to escape from it—at least temporarily, for she was no fool and she knew that she would not be able to escape forever. She would deal with those challenges tomorrow, but for tonight, she would simply pray and go to sleep.

∽

When Alice awoke early the next morning, she decided to give Vera a call even though it was Sunday. She and Vera usually did not walk on Sundays, because they were often busy with last-minute preparations for Sunday school or whatnot.

"Of course I want to walk," said Vera without missing a beat. "How else will I ever hear what's going on over there? I saw you and Mark walk by my house yesterday. You were so immersed in your conversation with him that you didn't even see me wave. Then the next thing I knew you were practically running back home. I've got to hear what on earth has happened."

So they met and walked and Alice talked. Although she could not make complete sense of her troubles with Adam and Mark, she did feel better when she had finished. Vera had raised two children of her own and had some sage advice about young adults to offer.

"Sure, they think they're all grown up," she told Alice, "or they want you to think they are, but underneath they are scared to death."

"Scared?"

"You know, of failing. They're old enough to realize that getting from where they are now to where they want to be may not be as easy as they had hoped. And it scares them. Overwhelms lots of them. Haven't you heard of the throngs of twenty-something kids that have returned to the nest?"

"Yes, but I guess I never thought about why that is. To be honest, I don't remember feeling like that. I just wanted to come home to help take care of my father. It had nothing to do with being scared."

"Well, maybe you're just different," teased Vera.

"Thanks a lot."

"I'm guessing that Adam is scared about a lot of things. I mean big things like life and death."

"I'm sure you're right," she told Vera when they reached the inn. "Now that I've had my therapy session, what do I owe you?"

"Hey, you've already paid me by telling me what's going on," said Vera. "Now I don't have to mug you after services to get the scoop."

Well, one thing Alice could trust about Vera was that even if she did "get the scoop" she was very discreet about keeping it to herself. Alice knew that her story was safe with her friend.

"Good morning," said Mark as Alice came into the inn. "Been walking?"

"Yes, as a matter of fact."

"Feeling better?"

"Oh yes," she told him. "I feel much better. Jane insisted I go right to bed last night. At the time I felt bad about doing so, but I think she was right."

"Well, you'd had quite a day." He lowered his voice. "What with the missing girl and Adam's shenanigans."

She smiled at the use of that old-fashioned word. "I better go get cleaned up so that I can help Jane with breakfast."

He nodded. "And I am about to take a walk myself." He peered out the window. "What a great morning for it too."

As she hurried up the stairs, she wondered if she should have asked him about Adam, and whether they should invite him to church or not. Well, that was Mark's concern, she told herself as she hurried to shower. After all, Sunday was a day of rest. Perhaps that is just what she needed today. No more "babysitting" teenaged girls or willful young adults. Today, she would enjoy church, family and friends, and let someone else take care of the problems.

"How are you feeling?" asked Jane when Alice came into the kitchen.

"Great," said Alice. "Thanks for the remedy."

Jane giggled. "I guess that's what we'll have to call it from now on. Whenever a sister is ready to lose it, we'll just recommend 'the remedy' and we'll all know what we mean."

Alice went to work slicing fresh strawberries and bananas. It was not long until Louise joined them and was put to work supervising the waffle iron.

"I couldn't resist," said Jane. "I'll make Laura whatever she would like, but I thought the other guests shouldn't be deprived."

Louise poured a ladle full of batter onto the hot iron. "I saw the Langleys on my way down. Mr. Langley looked fit as a fiddle. He said he had never felt better."

Alice smiled. "Perhaps this will be a good day for everyone."

"I certainly hope so." Louise gave Alice a funny look,

almost as if she wanted to ask her about what was going on, but Alice was thankful that she did not.

Alice was tempted to eat breakfast in the kitchen, something they all felt comfortable doing when there was a full house and the table was filled with guests. But knowing that Mark would wonder at her absence, she decided it would be better to simply go out and sit down. She reminded herself to hold her tongue, especially when it came to Adam.

To her relief, all went well at breakfast. When Louise offered the general invitation to the chapel that was always given guests on Sunday mornings, Alice was surprised that Mark spoke for both himself and Adam. "We plan to be there, don't we, Adam?"

Adam frowned, but nodded as if this had been previously arranged and not open to debate, and Alice began to clear the table.

"So far, so good," said Jane as she joined her in the kitchen. "Maybe Mark's little speech got through to our young man."

"Little speech?" Alice cringed at the thought of Adam being lectured because of her hurt feelings. That certainly wouldn't help anything.

"Yes," said Jane. "I missed it, but Louise filled me in last night. Apparently, Mark really laid into his godson."

"Oh dear."

"Now, don't worry about it. Louise thought it was quite appropriate, as did Aunt Ethel. And they're the only ones in this family who've actually raised kids, so maybe they know a thing or two."

"Maybe," said Alice, but she wasn't so sure. If anything, she anticipated that Adam would dislike her more than ever now. And, honestly, who could blame him? *Oh dear, she thought, I am in serious need of divine help on this problem.*

Chapter  Eleven

Alice and Louise walked over to the chapel early. Louise wanted to warm up on the organ, and Alice was meeting with her middle school girls church group before the service. Called "the ANGELs," an acronym for something only Alice and the girls knew, the group was in charge of dispensing the palms since this was Palm Sunday. Alice had planned a little talk for the girls, because last year they had discovered that the palms were useful in whacking the heads of boys in the congregation. Alice wanted to ensure that no head-whacking occurred today.

It was a lovely service. Alice never grew tired of hearing the Easter story, of Jesus' triumphal ride into Jerusalem and the way the people heralded Him as King.

As she left the chapel, Alice realized that she was feeling better than she had in days. Perhaps her problems with Adam would be resolved. Then she caught the look Adam gave her as she made her way toward the sidewalk, and the ache in her heart returned. She could see the obvious dislike in his eyes and, even more upsetting, she was afraid that her eyes reflected the feeling right back at him. No matter that she knew he was hurting and that he needed unconditional acceptance, she could not control her feelings. For the first time in her adult life, she felt almost as if she were the same emotional age as one of her ANGELs; for a moment she longed to grab one of those palms and whack Adam on the head.

She had complimented Rev. Kenneth Thompson on his fine sermon, visited with all her friends and was finally ready to go home when Mark came over and took her hand. "I hope that you have time in your busy schedule to join me for lunch," he said with a bright smile.

"Well, of course." She returned his smile, relieved that he had finally been able to break away from Ethel, who had taken him around to show off to all her friends.

"I thought we'd drive into the hills a bit. Are you up for a drive?"

"Certainly." She smiled.

"Good. Can you be ready to go soon?"

"Shall I change?" she asked. "Is this a formal or informal lunch?"

"Informal," he said. "I told Adam we'd try to get in a little hiking. I think it would be good for him."

She nodded slowly as the realization sunk in. This was not a date. This was a group outing. Still, it was too late to back out gracefully, and, besides, she told herself, why should she?

She hurried up to her room and put on jeans and a denim shirt with a tan sweatshirt over it, just in case there was a chill in the air, and then her walking shoes. *I can do this,* she told herself, *I can do this.*

"Where are you going?" asked Jane as she saw Alice emerging from her room with a determined look in her eye.

"With Mark and Adam," she said. "For lunch and a hike."

Jane stifled a giggle. "You sound like a Marine sergeant, Alice."

"That's because I'm trying to convince myself that *I can do this*," she said in a hup-two-three kind of voice. "*I can do this.*"

"Well, I hope you're right. If not, there's always 'the remedy.'"

Alice smiled. "You know, that's quite consoling, little sister."

Jane nodded. "Hey, get your comfort where you can. In the meantime, have fun and don't let him get to you."

"Mark?" asked Alice in an innocent voice.

"Yeah, you bet." Jane gently thumped her sister on the head. "You know who I mean."

"Right." Alice nodded. "I can do this."

Like a mantra, Alice mentally repeated that phrase as they got into Mark's Range Rover. *I can do this—I can do this—I can do this.* She was surprised that these were not the first words out of her mouth when Mark offered her a stick of gum.

"Uh, yes, thanks," she muttered, feeling somewhat dimwitted as he held the pack before her with a questioning expression.

"You okay?" he asked.

She smiled and nodded. "Yes, just thinking about something else."

"You all set back there?" he asked Adam as he started the engine.

Alice heard Adam muttering something back but could not quite make it out. Probably it made no difference since he was not talking to her anyway.

"Is that so?" said Mark.

Now her ears perked up a bit. What had she missed? Mark was looking at her with an expression that suggested he expected some kind of response on her part.

"Did I miss something?" she asked.

"Adam just mentioned that he gets carsick in the back-seat," said Mark.

"Oh." Alice turned to look at Adam and noticed that he seemed to be smirking. "Well, I don't mind sitting in back," she said.

Mark looked torn. "You don't get carsick, do you?"

She smiled. "Never have before." She was already opening the door. They quickly switched seats, and although she knew it was foolish, she felt as if she had been one-upped by Adam. Once she had taken her place in the back seat, it seemed as if their roles had been reversed, and she was suddenly the youth and the two adults were sitting up front.

Mark tried to include her in his comments, mostly about the region and various hiking trails and sites, but every time she attempted to engage in the conversation it seemed that she was either cut off or frozen out by Adam. Finally, she decided to focus her attention on the scenery that was flashing by the window. The ride reminded her of when she was a child, before Mother had passed away, and her family would take day trips to the mountains.

She smiled to herself as she remembered how her prim and proper older sister never wanted to get dirty or muss her hair, whereas Alice had been a bit of a tomboy. She had not minded baiting a hook or gathering firewood or wading through a creek to catch crawdads. Even the bugs and snakes had not worried her. She just thought they were interesting.

Her father appreciated these qualities, but Louise would sometimes tease her by calling her Al, and Mother would get concerned if Alice carried the dungarees and flannel shirts too far. "Don't forget you are a lady," Mother would counsel her, "and a pretty one at that." Of course, Alice had never considered herself pretty, with her red hair and freckles. Oh, her eyes were nice and people always told her she had a sweet, pleasant face, but pretty? No, she wouldn't go that far. Now Jane and Mother, they were the pretty ones—beauties really, and Louise had always possessed rather handsome good looks.

Alice wondered why she was thinking about all of this now. It was not the sort of thing that normally occupied her thoughts. Perhaps it was because she was supposed to be on something of a date. But was it really? Here she was sitting in the backseat, for the most part overlooked. She wondered now if it would have made any difference if she had not come at all. Furthermore, she wished that she had not. She would have been happier at home with her sisters than riding in the backseat with a surly young man taking her place up front. Suddenly, she wondered if she might too get carsick and actually had to suppress the urge to say, "Are we almost there?"

She looked back out the window, reminding herself that she was an adult, and then hummed hymns quietly, harmonizing with the sound of the tires on the curving mountain road.

"First stop, Cutter's Pass," said Mark as he parked the Range Rover in a small parking area. "I thought we could have a little hike to work up our appetites and then there's a café down the way where we can have lunch."

Adam climbed out of the car and stretched lazily. "I haven't hiked since Boy Scouts," he said to Mark. "Not sure if I'll be able to keep up." He looked longingly at the front seat. "Maybe I should just wait here."

"Nothing doing," said Mark. "We came to hike, and hike we will."

"Surely you can keep up with two old fogies like us," said Alice, instantly wishing she had not spoken when she noticed the frown shadowing Adam's face.

Mark laughed. "That's right, Adam. We're three times as old as you. I think that definitely gives you the advantage."

"Yeah, whatever."

"It's a beautiful day." Not taking any chances, Alice directed this comment to Mark. "Unseasonably warm for April."

Mark nodded. Soon they were off, and although Adam complained a bit at the start, he had no problem keeping up, and it was not long before Alice noticed that not only was he keeping up, but he also seemed to be driving them faster. They were going up a steady incline when she paused to catch her breath and remove her sweatshirt. It was much warmer than she had expected.

"You okay?" Mark called back to her. Adam was ahead of Mark, standing at the top of the rise now with his hands on his hips as if he was becoming impatient. From where he stood, looking down on Alice, it almost seemed a set up to show off his physical stamina and superiority. Maybe that was just her imagination. She wondered if fatigue could possibly give way to paranoia.

"I'm fine," she called up the hill as she tied the arms of the sweatshirt around her waist. "Just a bit too warm." She considered telling them to go on ahead without her, but that might suggest defeat or that she was too old and feeble to keep up with them. For whatever reason, maybe the competitive tomboy still residing within her older woman's body, she was simply not willing to give in.

"I can do this," she muttered aloud as she continued

walking uphill. But as she said it, she could hear her breaths coming out in short quick gasps and she knew her feet were dragging. Even though she had on her best walking shoes, she was getting a hot spot on her big right toe, which would probably become a blister if she didn't take care.

When she reached the top of the second rise, she paused in the shade to catch her breath and wipe the perspiration from her brow. That is when she noticed that Mark had on some sort of a safari hat and Adam was wearing his ball cap, actually facing forward now. They were both somewhat shielded from the noonday sun. She wished she had thought to bring along a hat or at least apply some sunscreen. Why hadn't she planned better?

"How are you holding up?"

She forced a smile to her lips. "Not as well as you two."

Mark pulled a handkerchief from his pocket and wiped a stream of sweat from his face. "Maybe we should slow down a little." He turned to Adam. "What do you think?"

Adam made a disappointed face. "I was just starting to enjoy this."

"That's okay," said Alice. "I'll be fine. How about if we just go at our own pace. If I get tired, I'll sit down and wait for you guys to come back for me."

"Are you sure?" asked Mark.

She nodded. "Yes, it's lovely out here. I would be happy to go at a more leisurely pace and simply enjoy all this natural beauty. I've barely had time to admire the wildflowers yet."

He smiled. "Okay, then."

It was not long before Mark and Adam were out of sight, but this did not bother Alice in the least. In fact, she was relieved. She stopped by a stream and removed her shoes, allowing her hot, tired feet a refreshing soak in the icy water.

She splashed some on her face and even considered drinking, but she knew that would not be wise. Too bad she hadn't thought to bring a water bottle.

Finally, her feet felt like ice cubes and even the hotspot seemed a bit better. She looked around until she spotted a nice big log that could serve as a handy bench. She had just put her socks back on when she heard a buzzing sound around her head. When she looked up, she saw a number of yellow jackets diving right at her. She grabbed her shoes and leapt to her feet, swinging her arms like a windmill as she attempted to fend off the angry little beasts. But it was too late. She suddenly felt a hot stinging sensation on her left forearm and then another on her right hand. She saw one wasp coming straight at her face. Panicking, she actually threw a shoe at it. Of course, that did no good. She missed the insect, but it did not miss her, and the flying shoe landed right in the stream where it began floating away like a little white raft.

With her remaining shoe in hand and yellow jackets still coming at her, Alice began to run along the stream, hoping to catch the wayward shoe, but after about fifty feet she realized she was running a losing race. She gave up and just shook her head sadly. She wanted to cry, but would not give in to her emotions. "You are a registered nurse," she told herself. "You know how to handle emergencies." Her hand, arm and cheek were all throbbing from the stings.

She looked about for anything that might help her and noticed the mud along the edge of the stream. She remembered that Native Americans had used mud poultices for healing. She scooped up some mud and applied it to the welts. The cool sticky substance, she found, was somewhat soothing. Now, she wondered, what could she do about the missing shoe? First, she knew that she should get back to the trail in case Mark and Adam had already turned back. She suspected that was unlikely since Adam had been so miraculously transformed into a mountain goat, but she did not want to miss them on the trail.

As she walked in her soggy socks toward the trail, she chided herself for being critical of Adam. What was wrong with her that she would feel like this toward an unfortunate young man who had lost both parents and was probably suffering from genuine depression? Just what kind of person was she anyway? Once she reached the trail, she found a rock and carefully examined it for wildlife. Finding it clear of danger, she sat down, looked at her remaining shoe and just sighed. One shoe is not good for anything. She thought that she probably should have thrown it into the stream too, then perhaps it would meet its mate and someone might find a pair of shoes. But that seemed like littering. She wished she had thought to make fresh poultices before she came back to the trail. The old ones were getting warm and dry now, but she left them on with the hope that the drying mud would absorb some of the yellow jacket venom. Fortunately, she was not allergic to stings. She would have been in trouble if that were the case; she had treated a boy in the hospital who almost died of anaphylactic shock from being stung just once. Alice was grateful that the yellow jackets had not gone into a full-scale rampage and swarmed her. She knew that even people who were not allergic could die from multiple stings. She paused to say a prayer of thanks. She knew that, despite her somewhat regrettable straits, He was still watching out for her.

She wondered why things had gone the way they had today. Was it Adam's fault? No, she knew it was not fair to blame the boy for her own carelessness. One should look before one sits—especially in the woods. Nevertheless, it did annoy her that Adam had been pushing them too hard. Even Mark had appeared exhausted when he paused to catch his breath. Still, Alice knew he would do what he could to keep up, especially if he felt that this was helping Adam—perhaps just the sort of connection Adam needed right now.

All that was fine and good, but why, she wondered, had she come along today? So far, it only seemed to be a lesson in pain and misery for her. And, of course, a blow to her pride. Tomboy indeed! She would much rather be at home, putting her feet up and having a nice cool lemonade on the front porch and visiting with guests. "Alice!" called Mark from up the trail.

She waved her one walking shoe from where she was seated. She felt pitiful and embarrassed for her sorry condition. Mark was actually jogging toward her now. Adam merely walked. "What's happened? Are you okay? What's on your face?"

She attempted a smile and then related her encounter with the yellow jackets, the loss of the shoe, and finally why she was slathered in mud. She could tell that Mark was caught between feeling concern and wanting to laugh.

"Go ahead and laugh," she told him. "I'm sure that I must be a sight."

By now Adam had joined them and he just stared at Alice as if she had two heads. But when Mark started laughing, Alice could not help herself and she began laughing too. Then she described how it had felt to see her walking shoe floating down the stream and the two of them were laughing so hard that she had tears streaming down her cheeks.

"Old people," said Adam. Then rolling his eyes, he turned and continued going down the trail.

First Alice felt somewhat stunned by Adam's complete lack of compassion. Then she saw Mark's perplexed face, and she just threw back her head and laughed even harder.

"Young people," she said, but not loud enough for Adam, who had already walked quite a way down the trail, to hear.

Mark nodded. "You said it." Then he helped her to her feet. "Do you think you can walk in your socks?" he asked with concern.

"Fortunately, I wore a thick pair," she said. "At least it's mostly downhill."

"I could go back to the car and drive ahead to see if I could find you some shoes," he said.

She smiled. "Now where do you think you would find a pair of size eight shoes out here? I'll be fine."

So they took the hike back slowly, pausing to allow Alice to rest her feet, which truly were feeling worse for wear. It was nearly three o'clock when they reached the Range Rover. Alice slid thankfully into the backseat and removed her ruined socks.

"How are your feet?" asked Mark as he started the engine.

"They've been better."

"That took you guys forever," complained Adam. "I thought I was going to have to call out the search and rescue."

"Well, that would have added another dimension to the adventure," said Alice with a tired smile.

"Man, I can't believe you actually threw your shoe in the creek," said Adam in a disgusted tone that sounded as if he were addressing a three-year-old. "That's like so totally lame."

"Yes," said Alice, "and that's how I feel too—lame."

"Are you hungry?" asked Mark.

"I'm starving," said Adam.

"How about you, Alice?"

"I'm hungry, but I don't think any respectable restaurant will let me in. Not in this condition."

"That's right," said Adam. "No shirts, no shoes, no service."

Alice sighed.

"Well, the place I'm taking you is at a lodge," said Mark. "They have a little gift shop. Maybe you can clean up and find some sort of footwear there."

As it turned out, the lodge had everything Alice needed. She purchased a pair of flip-flops, the kind that teens wear, with little palm trees on the sole, a periwinkle T-shirt with the logo of the lodge and a small packet of Advil, which she hoped would reduce the swelling of her bites and ease the pain in her feet. She even found some peach-scented lotion to soothe her irritated skin. And after about ten minutes in the ladies room, she emerged looking somewhat civilized, except for the big red welt on her cheek. *A battle scar*, she told herself.

"There you are," said Mark as he met her in the lobby. "I just talked the manager of the restaurant into staying open long enough for us to get something to eat. They normally close at three until the dinner hour, but I explained your circumstances and he took pity on us."

"Yeah," said Adam. "And I told him that I was starving."

Alice nodded without speaking. Maybe that is how she would get through the rest of their "outdoor adventure" trip. Just smile and nod, like those silly little bobble-head car ornaments that she had just seen in the gift shop.

Chapter  Twelve

W hat on earth happened to you?" cried Jane when Alice walked into the inn later that afternoon. "You look absolutely awful."

Alice forced a smile. "Thanks a lot."

Jane peered at the stings on Alice's swollen cheek and arm and then frowned. "Seriously, Alice, you're a mess."

"Yes, well, it's been an interesting day."

"She's a trooper," said Mark as he came in behind her. Adam pushed his way past the two of them, then headed straight up the stairs without saying a word of greeting to anyone.

Jane put her arm around Alice's shoulders. "Looks like you're in need of 'the remedy.'"

"The what?" Mark looked confused.

"Never mind," said Jane as she began ushering Alice upstairs.

"I'm sorry about everything," called Mark from behind her.

"That's okay," said Alice. "As I said, it was my own silly fault."

Alice gave Jane the shortened version of her disastrous

hike, and by the time they reached the third floor Jane was in stitches. "You really threw a shoe?"

"They were my favorite walking shoes too," Alice sighed as she reached for her doorknob.

"Hey, that's pretty cool footwear you're sporting right now," said Jane as she noticed Alice's colorful flip-flops.

Alice chuckled. "Actually, they're starting to grow on me. Honestly, with the shape my feet are in, I probably couldn't fit into regular shoes anyway. I think I should soak my feet in ice water."

"I'll bring some up for you," said Jane. "And some cortisone cream while I'm at it. We have some in the first aid kit downstairs."

"Thanks."

Alice felt like an eight-year-old again, as if she were incapable of caring for herself and was in need of special attention. Maybe she was. Anyway, she was not about to argue with Jane. Just going up the two flights of stairs had made her tender feet throb even more than the last leg of that ill-fated hike.

By the time she emerged from her shower, Jane had already set out a pan of ice water right in front of Alice's easy chair. The cortisone cream was on the little side table, along with a note instructing Alice to remain in her room and have dinner up there. *Unless you insist on coming down*, stated the final sentence.

Alice laughed. *Not on your life.*

She applied the cream to her stings and was instantly reminded of the year that she and Louise had gone to summer camp. She had been ten at the time and not happy about being away from home for two weeks. Once there, Alice had almost immediately broken out in a rash from contact with poison ivy. At first she thought it the perfect excuse to return to Acorn Hill since she was desperately homesick already, but the camp nurse assured her that they had treated many a case of poison ivy and had not lost a camper yet. The nurse was very nice. Funny, Alice hadn't thought about that incident for years.

Just as Alice leaned back into her easy chair, Wendell pushed open the door, which had been ajar, and with tail held high strutted into her room. She smiled at him as she patted her lap, and he jumped up and quickly made himself comfortable. There she sat, soaking her feet in the cold water for nearly an hour, dozing off and on, as the cat purred happily in her lap.

"Ready for some supper?" asked Louise, coming in with a tray.

Alice opened her eyes and smiled. "Yes, thank you. That's very thoughtful of you and Jane. I honestly don't know if I could have made it back down the stairs and then up again. I think I've done enough climbing for one day."

Louise chuckled. "Yes, Jane filled me in. Aren't you a bit old for that sort of nonsense?" She cleared the side table next to Alice, then set the tray on it.

"Actually, I had been thinking I was in pretty good shape," admitted Alice. "That is, until today. Now I feel as if I'm a hundred years old."

"I heard that Adam gave you and Mark a run for your money." Louise sat down on the bed, folding her arms across her front as she waited for Alice to taste the soup.

"*Mmm*, Jane's tomato bisque is the best."

Louise cleared her throat. "Adam is downstairs right now. He is telling Laura about how you slowed them down on their hike this afternoon, and how they almost missed lunch because of you."

Alice sighed. "That figures."

"He is the rudest young man."

"I shouldn't have gone with them today," said Alice. "It should've just been a special time for Mark and Adam, a guys' trip, you know. Adam is right. I did ruin the day for them."

"*Humph.* It sounds more like Adam ruined the day for you."

"I'm just not sure how I fit in," said Alice as she set her spoon down.

"What do you mean?"

"Oh, with Mark, I guess."

"But how could you possibly know? It seems that all this trouble with Adam is quite a distraction for you and Mark. That is, if your plan was to spend time with him. By the way, did you know that Mark has an appointment with Richard Watson this week?"

Alice's eyes grew wide—Richard Watson was a local real estate agent. "Seriously?"

Louise nodded. "Richard told me as much himself at church this morning."

"Mark is planning to do some real estate shopping?"

"So it seems. Richard said that Mark set it up with him soon after he got into town. Apparently he saw a for sale sign in front of the old Olsen house as he was driving by and thought it looked like a worthwhile investment."

"That is a darling house," said Alice as she pictured the small white cottage in her mind's eye. "Of course, it's a bit run down, but it could be very sweet if fixed up properly. And the rose garden was always lovely. I suspect that there might still be some bushes surviving amongst the weeds."

Louise nodded as she stood. "Well, I should get back down to help Jane with dinner. Mark and Adam are going to join us again tonight."

Alice frowned as she looked down at her puffy red feet. "I feel like a naughty child who's been banished to her room for the evening."

Louise laughed as she paused in the doorway. "That's not too far from the truth. But that's only because you failed to remember your age today, my dear."

"I don't think I'll do that again."

"I certainly hope not."

"Please make my apologies to Mark, and uh, Adam too."

"*Humph.* I will tell Mark, but I don't think I will be making any apologies to Adam."

Louise went back downstairs, and Alice was left to her quiet dinner and continued foot-soaking. She actually welcomed this bit of solitude. Too much had been going on these past few days, and now, more than ever, she felt the need for some quiet time. Lounging in pajamas, reading her mystery and going to bed early sounded like the perfect prescription for her. Maybe Louise was right. Maybe she was getting old.

∞

Fortunately, Alice felt more like herself the following morning. She awoke earlier than usual and was surprised that she was actually able to get her feet into her loafers. They were still a bit sore, but much better than yesterday. Even so, she was not sure that she wanted to walk with Vera today. She decided to give her good friend a call. Alice slowly made her way downstairs to the phone at the reception desk, feeling each step in her sore muscles and feet.

"I hope you're not seriously injured," said Vera after Alice had briefly explained her condition.

Alice laughed. "My only serious injury was to my pride, Vera. It is painfully clear that I'm no spring chicken."

"Who wants to be?"

"Well, I'd just be glad not to feel like I'm a hundred and three today."

"So when will we be walking again?"

"I'll let you know. Maybe tomorrow if we take it easy. But first I'll have to get some new walking shoes."

Vera laughed. "And no more using them as projectiles."

After hanging up the phone, Alice went into the kitchen where she discovered Jane already puttering about.

"Smells good," said Alice as she eyed the nicely browned loaf that was cooling on the butcher-block countertop. "Banana nut loaf?"

"I thought it would be nice to have it warm for breakfast." Jane regarded Alice closely. "How're you feeling?"

"Better, I think."

"I stopped by your room last night, but you were sound asleep."

"I was pretty worn out."

Jane rolled her eyes. "Imagine that."

"Yes, I know," said Alice. "Louise already gave me the lecture."

"You mean to start acting your age instead of your shoe size?"

Alice nodded as she poured herself a cup of tea. "Funny thing is that I've been feeling about the same age as my shoe size lately."

"Oh well," said Jane, "no harm in being young at heart."

"*Yoo-hoo*," sang out Ethel as she opened the back door.

"Hello, Auntie," called Jane.

"I had to pop in and see how Alice's date with Mark went yesterday."

"Date?" Alice frowned. "It wasn't exactly a date."

"Well, whatever you young people call it."

Alice had to laugh. "*Young people!*"

Ethel went for a cup of coffee. "Well, younger than some of us." She sat down across from Alice. "Go ahead," she said. "Tell Auntie everything."

So for the third time, Alice told about the unfortunate hiking trip, trying to do a condensed version, but when she failed to embellish it properly, Jane took over and very dramatically reenacted the whole thing until all three of them were laughing so hard that they had tears running down their faces.

"Is that what *really* happened?" asked Ethel as she wiped her eyes.

"Well, Jane *is* given to exaggeration," said Alice.

"Creative license," said Jane.

"Oh my." Ethel just shook her head. "I don't think I'd call that a date either, dear."

"No, I'd call it a catastrophe." Alice reconsidered this. "Although, our late lunch was actually rather nice. And I have to say that Mark was entirely gracious and kind throughout everything."

"How about the boy?" Ethel peered at Alice with undisguised curiosity.

"Well . . ."

"He was a complete brat," said Jane, "and he wasn't much better last night either."

"Oh dear," said Alice. "What did he do?"

"Well, for starters, he took Laura off without even talking

to her parents—just whisked her away after dinner without telling anyone. Needless to say, they were quite upset."

"Oh my."

"And then he and Mark got into an argument about it."

"Poor Mark."

"Yes," agreed Jane. "I have to give it to Mark, he was surprisingly patient with that surly young man, but I could tell that he wanted to throttle him."

"Someone *should* throttle him," said Ethel.

"Are you volunteering?" Jane pointed a wooden spoon at her aunt.

Ethel chuckled. "Wouldn't be the first time I set a young person in his rightful place."

"I can vouch for that," said Alice.

"Morning, girls," called Louise as she came into the kitchen. "I see the party has already begun."

"Isn't it nice having Alice home this week?" said Jane.

"It's a good thing too," said Alice, "Since I'm sure I would've been completely useless at the hospital right now."

"So what are your plans today?" asked Louise as she poured herself a cup of coffee and sat down across from Ethel.

Alice shrugged. "I'm not sure, well, other than that I won't be taking any hikes. I would like to get to Potterston to shop for a new pair of walking shoes."

"Hello?" called a masculine voice. Mark pushed open the door to the kitchen. "Are males allowed in here?"

Jane laughed. "Only you, Mark. Come on in."

"That is correct," said Louise. "You are special."

"Thanks." He smiled at Alice. "How are you doing today?"

"Much better, thanks."

"Coffee?" offered Jane.

He nodded and took a chair across from Alice. "I am so sorry for every—"

"As I said," she told him, "it wasn't your fault. I brought it on myself."

"I shouldn't have let Adam push us so much," he said, then groaned as he rubbed the top of his legs. "Believe me, I'm paying for it too."

Alice felt selfishly relieved at this admission. "Well, I suppose we're not as young as we used to be."

"You're telling me." He shook his head. "I could barely make it down the stairs without screaming in pain just now."

Alice laughed. "Well, I would recommend some ibuprofen for starters. And then perhaps a hot soak in the tub might help."

"And that's your professional opinion?"

"Well, that and don't let Adam push you around so much."

The other women actually gave a little applause for this.

"I know," said Mark. "It's awful, isn't it? I feel so terrible about how things went last night with Laura. I'm considering giving Adam his walking papers today."

"Oh, Mark," began Alice. "You don't really want to—"

"I don't see why not. He doesn't seem to appreciate anything and it's clear that he doesn't want to be here. All he does is stir up trouble."

"But it's only because he's feeling so—"

"I don't buy that, Alice," he said in a firm voice. "I mean, I realize that he's hurting about his parents, but that certainly doesn't give him the right to make everyone else miserable."

"That's true," said Louise.

"We're all mature adults," said Jane. "We ought to be able to come up with something that will get through to this young man."

"You mean besides my throttling him?" said Ethel.

Alice made an apologetic smile to Mark. "She offered."

"Not a bad idea."

"Can't you just give him a little more time?" asked Alice, surprised that she was actually feeling sorry for Adam now. The idea of Mark asking him to leave the inn was unsettling.

"Maybe I can give him a warning," said Mark, "that he can either shape up or ship out."

"Yes," agreed Alice. "That sounds fair."

"Now, not to change the subject," said Jane, "but, Alice, would you mind picking up a couple of things for me if you go to Potterston today?"

"Not at all."

"You're going to Potterston?" asked Mark.

"To purchase some new walking shoes." She grinned at him. "For some reason I find myself in need."

"Want some company?"

"Sure."

"Though I do have an appointment this morning," he said. "Do you mind waiting until after that? I should be back by eleven."

"That's fine."

"And, considering that you may still be recovering from that horrible hike yesterday, perhaps I should drive you."

"That would be great." Then she considered something worrisome, but hated to ask.

"Something wrong?" he asked.

"Well, I was just wondering . . . uh, do you plan to invite Adam to join us today?"

He laughed. "Ah, not this time."

"Oh." She hated that she felt so relieved.

"I'll give you my list after breakfast," said Jane. "Most of all I want you to go by Gierson's and get lots of eggs. They're having a great special and you know we need a bunch for the egg hunt."

"You use real eggs?" asked Mark.

"Of course," said Louise, "and everyone at the inn is invited to an egg-dyeing party on Friday afternoon."

"Sounds like fun," said Mark. "Count me in."

Chapter ❧ Thirteen

Alice had to admit that she enjoyed riding in the front seat this time. It felt nice to be a grownup sitting next to Mark as he drove them to Potterston. Their conversation was light and comfortable, carried mainly by Mark as he related several exciting stories about his practice at the zoo.

"You are quite a storyteller," she said. She wanted to ask him about his appointment with Richard Watson and whether he liked the Olsen house, but since he did not mention anything about it, she thought that perhaps he would prefer that she didn't know. Still, she was curious about what he was planning.

"I spoke to Adam this morning," said Mark.

"How did it go?"

He shook his head. "Not too well. Adam immediately got quite defensive. He said that if I didn't want him around that he might as well just clear out."

"Oh dear."

"I assured him that I wanted him around but that I wanted him to be more courteous to others."

"Could he understand that?"

"I'm not sure. He acted as if he hadn't done much

wrong. It's almost as if he wanted to push me, to see what I'd do about it." He scratched his beard. "If I didn't know better, I'd say that Adam is testing me, but that seems ridiculous. Good grief, he's almost twenty years old. It's not as if I plan to act like a father to him. I just want to help him."

"I know you do, Mark."

"The thing is, Alice . . ." He paused to glance at her, then put his eyes back on the road. "I hate to admit this, but I really don't like Adam very much."

Alice did not know what to say. The truth was that she didn't either.

"I know that sounds horrible. It's certainly not a very Christian way to feel about someone, especially about the only son of your deceased best friend, as well as your own godson. But that's how I feel. If I were to meet Adam on the street, after all he's put me through, well, I probably wouldn't give him the time of day. Except that I feel responsible for him, you know?"

"I know."

"But I have to ask myself, just what exactly is my responsibility to him?"

"I'm not sure, Mark."

"I'm not sure either. I've considered what your father used to teach, that a godfather was responsible for a child's spiritual upbringing should the parents be unable. And while I agree with this, at least in theory, I have to wonder what I can possibly do to influence Adam now that he's all grown up. And do you know what really bugs me, Alice?"

"What?"

"I'm feeling angry at Gregory now. I feel that he must not have done a good job raising Adam. It feels horrible to think that, especially considering how much I loved Gregory." Mark sighed deeply.

"I can see that it's complicated."

"You said it."

Alice was relieved that they had arrived in Potterston now. Otherwise, she might have felt compelled to confess that she, too, disliked Adam. Somehow, she just did not want to admit that to Mark. It was bad enough that he was having problems with his feelings. At least Alice should try to appear to like the young man. As they walked into the shoe store, Alice decided to look for the good qualities in Adam. Surely, he must have some.

Alice found an excellent pair of walking shoes after only trying on a few pairs. "These are so comfortable," she said as she walked around the store, "that I don't want to take them off."

"You don't have to," said the pleased salesman. "I can ring them up for you and put your other shoes in the box."

"Perfect," said Alice.

After that, Mark insisted on treating Alice to lunch. "I know I can't make up for yesterday," he said after they were seated at a window table at a nice restaurant, "but I can try."

She waved her hand. "I think that the sooner we forget about all that the better we'll feel."

He nodded and looked down at the menu. Alice studied him from the other side of the table. He was such a kind and gracious man, and he treated her so well. What more could anyone hope for? Yet she was not sure—not only about her own feelings, but also about his. Perhaps it was better just to go on the way they were and be content that they were simply friends. They both decided to try out the special, a salmon soufflé with sautéed asparagus, and neither of them was disappointed.

"That was excellent," said Alice to Mark as the waiter removed their empty dishes.

"Dessert?" he asked.

"Oh, I shouldn't—" began Alice.

"Why not?" said Mark.

She smiled as she considered all the calories that she must have burned off yesterday. "Yes, why not?" They both ordered the crème caramel, which turned out to be delicious.

"We have similar tastes," observed Mark as they were leaving.

Alice nodded. "Except that you had coffee with your dessert and I had tea."

"Well, we wouldn't want the waiter to think we were boring." He smiled as he held the door for her.

"Thank you," she told him. "Lunch was just lovely."

Mark dropped off Alice at the grocery store. "Do you mind if I run some errands," he asked, "while you shop?"

"Not at all."

They agreed on how long it should take, and Alice took Jane's short list and went into the store. She piled her cart high with eggs, relieved to see that there was no limit on the special price. Then she gathered the other items and made her way to the checkout stand.

"Alice Howard?"

Alice turned to see a vaguely familiar face behind her. She smiled at the attractive woman in the periwinkle-blue jogging suit but still could not quite place her. "Yes?"

"Oh, I thought that was you." The woman smiled brightly. "Matilda Singleton," she said. "Or at least I used to be."

"Matilda Singleton?" Alice struggled to put this vaguely familiar face with the vaguely familiar name.

"We went to college together."

Alice nodded and smiled. "Oh yes, Matilda, of course. I remember you now."

The woman patted her platinum-colored hair and stood straighter. "Well, I have to admit that I've changed some. And I go by Mattie now."

"You look great," said Alice. It was true. Matilda, or Mattie, almost looked better now than she had back in college.

"Well, I finally lost that weight." Mattie patted her chin with the back of her hand, causing her assortment of gold bangle bracelets to jangle. "And then I got a little work done here and there. Just small things, you know. But every little bit helps when we get to be this age. Right?"

Alice nodded uncertainly as she moved her cart forward in the line. "Do you live around here, Mattie?"

"I just moved to Potterston last year," said Mattie. "My late husband Arnold grew up here and he'd always dreamed of retiring in his hometown. We'd barely moved into our condo when he suffered a cardiac arrest."

"Oh, I'm sorry."

Mattie did not look particularly upset. "Well, between you and me and the lamppost, I was about to divorce him anyway."

Unsure of how she should respond to that, Alice continued unloading her cart, placing carton after carton of eggs on the moving belt.

Mattie continued chattering at her as the cashier rang up Alice's groceries.

"Lotta eggs," said the young man. "You planning to make a giant omelet or something?"

Alice laughed. "Actually, we're going to boil and dye them for an Easter egg hunt."

"You're serious?" He blinked, then totaled the cost. "I didn't know people did stuff like that anymore."

"They do where I live." Alice gave him her money and waited.

"And where's that?" he asked as he gave her the change.

"Acorn Hill," she told him.

"Oh, you live in Acorn Hill," said Mattie as she began to unload her groceries onto the belt. "That's such a sweet little town. I tried to talk Arnold into settling down there but, oh no, he would have nothing to do with it. Potterston or nothing."

Alice noticed Mark coming in the store's entrance. "Need a hand?" he called as he got closer.

Alice smiled and waved him over. "Do you remember Mark Graves?" she asked Mattie as she returned her wallet to her purse.

"Is *that* Mark Graves?" cooed Mattie with obvious appreciation. "Well, he's still just as handsome as ever." Then she lowered her voice. "So you actually nabbed him after all. And here I'd heard that you two had broken up."

"Actually, we're just—"

"Mark Graves," called Mattie cheerfully. "I'll bet you don't remember me."

Mark and Alice waited for Mattie to complete her purchases, then the three of them chatted briefly near the exit. Finally, Mattie suggested that they should stow their groceries and meet at the coffee shop next to the grocery store. "We can keep talking about old times," she told them. "My treat."

Mark wheeled Alice's cart to the Range Rover and then opened the trunk. They decided the weather was cool enough that the eggs would be safe for a short visit.

"Do you remember her from when we were dating in college?" Alice asked as she handed Mark a bag to be placed in the back. "She was a casual friend of mine."

"Not exactly," he admitted. "The name sounds a bit familiar, but I don't really recall her face."

"Well, she's lost some weight and even admitted that she's had some, uh, work done."

Mark nodded knowingly as he closed the back of his car with a thud. "Went under the knife to look younger, eh? It's got to make you wonder."

"What?" Alice peered at him as they walked across the parking lot.

"Whether it's worth all that pain, money and danger. Any surgery has its risks. Why take the chance?"

"But she does look good, doesn't she?"

He shrugged, and suddenly Alice remembered something.

"I didn't get a chance to straighten her out," she said quickly as they walked toward the coffee shop. "Mattie, uh, well, she thinks we're married."

Mark chuckled. "She does, does she?"

"I was about to explain to her that we're not, but then she began chatting with you and I didn't get the—"

"Hello, you two," called Mattie as she joined them.

As Mark went to the counter to order, Alice filled Mattie in on her marital status.

"Oh, I see." Mattie's carefully penciled eyebrows lifted. "Well, isn't that something. Alice Howard never married and Mattie Singleton has been through four husbands already."

Alice felt her eyes growing wide. "*Four?*"

Mattie laughed. "That's right. I have to admit that those alimony checks came in handy, and then, of course, the insurance."

"Oh my."

"Now don't act as if it's so scandalous," said Mattie. "It's not as if all of the divorces were my fault. Well, other than the fact that I have the worst luck imaginable when it comes to picking good men, and just marriage in general."

Alice noticed her large diamond rings, one on each hand, and her glittering earrings. Mattie may have had bad luck with men, but it appeared that alimony and insurance money had paid off. Still, Alice did not believe that baubles were worth the heartache of failed relationships.

"There you go," said Mark as he set down the tray of coffee and tea on the small table and joined them.

"Mark Graves," said Mattie in an interested, if not slightly flirtatious, tone. "So, tell me, what have you been doing with yourself all these years?"

Mark smiled and then pleasantly indulged her with a short but impressive synopsis of his forty-year career in animal medicine, including mentions of his various travels.

"Fascinating," said Mattie. "I've traveled quite a bit myself. Two of my husbands were avid globetrotters. About ten years ago, I even went down the Amazon. My husband Richard booked us a cruise right down that river. I wasn't too sure about it. Fortunately, the cruise ship turned out to be quite luxurious, and I never even had to get off it if I didn't want to."

"A cruise ship on the Amazon?" Alice thought this sounded rather strange.

Mattie laughed. "Yes, it does seem a bit incongruous since the people who live down there are so primitive and impoverished. I suppose it was an interesting study in contrasts."

"And what have you been doing since college, Mattie?" asked Mark. "Well, other than cruising down the Amazon?"

Mattie smiled and launched into a descriptive tale about all the various places she had lived and all the unusual things she had done. Apparently, Mattie had only married rich men.

By the time Mattie finished, Alice felt exhausted. Of course, Mattie had not gone into too much detail about the careers or personalities of the four husbands, or their financial contribution to her affluent and exciting lifestyle, Alice noted. "Wow," said Mark. "That's quite impressive."

"Oh, it's not much compared to all that you've done," said Mattie in a flattering tone. "How fulfilling it must be for you to go around the world saving endangered animals. I feel rather selfish not to have pursued a career."

"Careers aren't everything," Mark assured her.

"Well, I guess I can't complain," she said. "At least I've seen and done a lot in my lifetime. I always tell my daughter whenever she complains that I'm traveling too much, you only live once and you might as well do it with flair."

"You've certainly done that," said Alice.

"How about you?" Mattie turned her attention to Alice now. "What have you been up to all these years?"

Alice felt that her life would sound dull and boring compared to what she had just heard, but she had no reason to make it seem bigger than it was. It was not as if she was ashamed of her life.

"Don't let Alice fool you," said Mark. "Acorn Hill is a delightful place to live. And, believe me, that so-called quiet little town of hers is full of all kinds of funny adventures and excitement."

"Oh, I don't know . . ."

"We do have our share of adventures," admitted Alice. "And it's rather nice living in a town where everyone knows you."

"And were you serious about what you said in the grocery store?" asked Mattie. "Do you really intend to boil all those dozens of eggs and then dye them for an Easter egg hunt?"

"That's right," said Alice. "My mother started doing this when Louise and I were just little girls, and I started it up again when I moved back to Acorn Hill. We've been doing it ever since. It has grown and has become a local tradition."

"Well, it sounds like fun. I might have to come over and see all this for myself," said Mattie.

"You're most welcome," said Alice.

"And then I can see your little inn too." Mattie nodded. "In fact, that's just what I think I'll do. I'll drive over next Saturday."

"Good," said Alice. "Perhaps you'd like to join us for dinner at the inn that night."

"Now that would be nice."

"Alice's sister Jane used to be a professional chef in San Francisco," said Mark. "You won't be disappointed."

"Well, this just gets better and better." Mattie smiled. "Please, count me in."

They visited a bit more, then Alice grew concerned about the eggs in the back of Mark's Range Rover. "We probably should get those groceries home," she said to Mark.

He nodded. "Yes, we sure don't want to take the chance of making anyone ill."

"See you on Saturday," called out Mattie.

Alice was not sure why she felt slightly down as Mark drove them back to Acorn Hill. It was not as if she was jealous of the exciting life that Mattie had led, and yet something about their conversation did trouble her.

"That Mattie is quite a gal," said Mark in a voice that sounded as if he was not so sure.

"She certainly has led an interesting life," agreed Alice.

"Although she doesn't really seem happy," he observed.

"You don't think so?" Alice considered this. "She puts on a good show of it. She's done and seen so much."

"Lots of people are like that, Alice. They try to make things seem bigger and brighter than they actually are. I guess it makes them feel better, even if it's only briefly."

"That is an interesting observation."

"That's what I like about you, Alice."

She turned and looked at him. "What?"

"You're the real deal."

She smiled. "The real deal?"

He nodded. "If you ask me, that's worth a whole lot more than all the diamonds and cruises in the world."

Chapter  Fourteen

O h good," said Jane as Alice and Mark brought in the groceries. "It looks as though you bought the eggs at the special price too. Goodness, I hope I cleared enough space in the refrigerator for them." She turned to Mark. "By the way, Adam's been asking when you were getting back."

He nodded. "Yes, I told him we'd do something together this afternoon. I better go find him now."

After he left, Jane told Alice that the Winstons had taken a day trip to the Amish country. "I think they were trying to get Laura away from Adam today," she admitted as she put away the last carton of eggs.

"Oh dear," said Alice. "I feel so bad when it seems that guests aren't feeling comfortable at the inn."

"Don't worry about it," said Jane. "It's not as if it's your fault."

Alice nodded. "I know you're right, but I just feel responsible. How did Laura seem?"

"Quiet." Jane checked her oven. "I felt sorry for her as her parents hauled her away. I mean, she's seventeen going on eighteen, in her last year of high school, and here she is stuck spending spring break with her parents in a town where the most lively activities include choir practice and quilting bees."

Alice frowned. "Poor Laura."

"It's no wonder that she likes hanging with Adam. At least he's closer to her age and they certainly seem to get along well."

"Although he's perhaps not the best influence."

"Maybe not." Jane pointed to Alice's new shoes. "Nice. How are your feet feeling?"

"Better. But I think I'll go upstairs and give them a rest." She glanced around the kitchen. "That is, unless, you need help with anything?"

"Nah, not much going right now. You go put your feet up."

"I was hoping to work on my quilt."

"Sounds like a plan."

Alice became so absorbed working on the baby quilt that she actually lost track of the passing hours. When she finally glanced at her clock, she saw that it was time for her to go down and help Jane with dinner preparations. She stood up and stretched. She wondered if Mark and Adam were back yet. Mark had hoped to join them for the evening meal. She freshened up and changed into an outfit she usually reserved for church. Jane thought that the caramel-colored sweater looked nice on Alice. She paused in front of her bureau mirror and remembered Mattie's words earlier today: "Every little bit helps when we get to be this age."

Alice's goal had always been to grow old gracefully, which to her meant allowing nature to take its course. She looked at her graying hair and slightly sagging chin and sighed. Under normal circumstances, these signs of aging did not trouble her in the least, but tonight they seemed more noticeable. She looked closer, wondering what had happened to the red-haired girl who used to be able to keep up with the boys. Then she smiled, knowing that the girl was still in there. After all, Alice's spirit had not aged at all. That was what really counted.

Alice headed down the stairs with a bit more bounce in her step.

"Oh, there you are," said Jane when they met on the second landing. "I was just doing a quick turndown and truffle drop."

"The old turndown and truffle drop," teased Alice. "Sounds like something an acrobat in the circus might do."

"Yes," said Jane. "I am quite spry for my age."

"Age . . ." Alice sighed. "I'm trying not to think about it too much. Isn't it just a number anyway?"

Jane laughed. "I should think you'd be feeling like a young girl these days, Alice, with Mark paying you all this special attention."

Alice was just about to tell Jane about Mattie when they reached the foyer and Jane paused to look at a large vase of yellow roses. "Where did these come from?"

Alice looked more closely at the roses. "They are beautiful, aren't they?"

"I'll say." Jane spotted a small white envelope tucked into the back of the arrangement. "They're from Wild Things. Oh, that must've been why I saw Craig Tracy's van on the street this afternoon. I was working in my herb bed." She handed Alice the card. "They're for you."

Alice recognized the handwriting on the envelope. The bouquet was from Mark. She pulled out a card and read the simple message.

Dear Alice,
  Sorry about yesterday's horrible hike.
                    Warmly,
                    Mark

"So what is it?" demanded Jane. "A proclamation of undying love? A proposal? An invitation to a secret marriage ceremony?"

Alice laughed. "Hardly." She handed Jane the note. "Just a sweet apology. Goodness, he didn't need to go to such trouble." Then she bent down to smell the flowers. "Although I do love yellow roses."

"Look," said Jane pointing to a single red rose. "There's one red one too." She thought a minute. "You know, Alice, yellow roses are symbolic of friendship, but red is supposed to be for true love. Do you think this bouquet is meant to have some sort of message?" Jane counted the roses. "Eleven yellows, and one red. *Hmmm?*"

"Maybe Craig was short on yellow roses," suggested Alice. "So he stuck in a red one to make a full dozen."

"That's unlikely. Roses usually come in to shops by the dozen. No, Alice, here's what I think," said Jane as they walked toward the kitchen. "I think that Mark is assuring you of his friendship, and that's important, but the single red rose is meant to be like a question mark—as if he's asking whether or not you still love him."

"Oh, I don't think . . ."

"Just consider it, Alice. It makes perfect sense."

They were in the kitchen now, and Alice turned to the sink to wash her hands, her regular practice before she helped Jane, but perhaps she was doing a bit more thorough job than usual. She knew it was an attempt to avoid Jane's prying questions. She truly didn't know the answers to Jane's questions. Did she love Mark as she did in college before they broke up to go their separate ways, he to his career and she to Acorn Hill and her father? She was very fond of Mark, but . . .

"Come on, Alice," said Jane as she pulled some things from the refrigerator. "Don't pretend to ignore me."

Alice turned around and looked at her younger sister. "I just really don't know, Jane. Mark and I haven't even talked about, well, us."

"That's because he's been so distracted by Adam."

Alice nodded. "That's true enough."

"Adam isn't exactly helping matters."

"Especially since it seems he can barely stand to be around me."

"Who can't stand to be around you?" asked Louise as she came into the kitchen. "Mercy, Alice, I'm sure that you must be imagining things. I don't believe I can think of a single person in Acorn Hill who doesn't love you."

"I'm speaking of Adam," said Alice.

"Oh." Louise nodded and sighed. "Yes, you may be right about that. I've tried to put that young man out of my head. He is certainly a troublemaker."

"Better watch ourselves," warned Jane. "I hear someone coming in the front door just now, and I'm expecting Mark and Adam to join us for dinner tonight."

The sisters started chatting about the latest goings on in town as they worked together to prepare a meal of ham and Jane's special recipe for herbed scalloped potatoes.

"Hello in there," called Mark a few minutes later as he peered in the kitchen door, as if he was afraid to enter.

"You're back," said Alice. "Come on in. I love the beautiful roses, Mark. Thank you."

"It was the least that I could do after your ordeal."

"Come sit down," said Jane. "Tell us about your afternoon."

"I just made a fresh pot of decaf," offered Louise. "Would you like some?"

Mark sighed as he eased himself into a chair. "That would be delightful."

"You sound tired," noted Alice.

"Exhausted," admitted Mark. "I'm too old to be trying to keep up with someone Adam's age."

"Then why are you?" asked Alice.

Mark thought about this as he stirred some cream into his coffee. "I'm not exactly sure. I guess I'm hoping that I'll make a connection with him somehow."

"So what did you do this afternoon?" asked Jane.

Mark laughed. "Believe it or not, we went go-cart racing. We drove past a place on the outskirts of Potterston where they have—"

"Crazy Jack's Racetrack?" exclaimed Jane. "You went there?"

Mark nodded. "Well, it seemed to spark something in Adam when he saw it. Suddenly he remembered the time when his dad and I took him racing about ten years ago. And so I decided to just take a chance. Of course, when I suggested it, his immediate response was that it was silly. Then I stupidly talked him into it." Mark exhaled loudly. "We ended up spending three hours there. I could barely pry myself out of the little car when we were done."

"But Adam enjoyed it?" asked Alice.

"Yes, sort of. As we were leaving, Adam noticed this scrawny kitten that kept meowing. The owner, Crazy Jack, I guess, said it was a stray that he was going to take to the pound. Adam was all over that kitten, saying that the people at the pound would kill it. I assured him that they would probably just give it some shots and some good food and find it a good home, but Adam wouldn't believe me."

"And?" Louise peered over her glasses at Mark.

"And . . . well . . . I hope it's okay, but Adam brought the kitten home. I mean to the inn."

"Oh, that's perfectly fine," said Alice.

"Yes, just tell him to watch out for Wendell," warned Jane.

"Maybe he should introduce them so Wendell doesn't do anything mean to the kitten," suggested Alice. "Wendell does seem to think he rules the house."

"We stopped by the pet store where we got all the necessary accessories, a collar, a bed and kitty litter. I can easily give him the shots and whatnot myself, although it was too late to stop by a vet clinic to get the serums." Mark set down his cup. "I know it isn't a good idea. I told Adam it made no sense for him to adopt a pet when he can barely take care of himself."

"That's true," said Louise.

"Naturally, that ended up in a big fight," said Mark. "Adam is probably in his room pouting now."

"Goodness," said Louise, "he really needs to get a grip on his emotions."

"It's really not that easy when you're depressed," said Alice.

"Maybe the kitten will help," suggested Jane.

Mark just shook his head. "I don't know. I actually feel sorry for the kitten. He might've gotten a good home if he'd been taken to the pound. He's rather cute, really, all black with four white paws. I can't quite imagine him enjoying living in Adam's car."

"Well, it's a step up from living on the street," said Jane.

"Is living in his car what Adam plans to continue doing?" asked Alice as she finished making the sauce for the brandied peaches to go with the ham.

"That's what he says."

"He doesn't want to continue his education?" asked Louise.

"No interest at all. He says it's a waste of time."

"Yeah," said Jane, removing the foil from the scalloped potatoes and slipping the pan back into the oven, "like living in your car's a great way to spend your days."

"Try to tell him that," said Mark.

⚭

When dinner was ready, the three sisters, Mark and Adam gathered around the table. Alice made a polite inquiry about Adam's new kitten, but his reply was so chilly that Alice was warned against further conversation with him.

"What's his name?" asked Jane as she passed Adam the breadbasket.

"Boots," said Adam. "At least for now. It's not the greatest name."

"I think it's cute," said Jane. "Mark told us that he has white feet."

Adam brightened. "He does. Maybe you'd like to see him after dinner."

Alice tried not to feel put out by the way Adam seemed to warm up to Jane. *At least he's engaging with someone, she assured herself. Even if it isn't me.*

"Is he eating well?" asked Louise. "We heard he was quite skinny."

"Mark said to only feed him small amounts at first," explained Adam, "and to feed him every couple of hours."

"How's it going?" asked Mark.

"He ate every bite," said Adam. "I think he wanted more, but I didn't give him any."

"Good," said Mark. "Too much could really make him sick."

Alice wanted to ask if Boots knew how to use the litter-box, but knew that she would not get much of a response. Instead, she asked Louise, "Do you remember the kitten we had as girls? Oliver?"

"Yes." Louise nodded. "Wasn't he black and white too?"

"That's what I recall," said Alice. "I think he had three white feet and a white nose."

"I remember him!" exclaimed Jane.

"Oh, I think not," said Louise. "You weren't born when we got him."

"I remember a big, old cat named Oliver," insisted Jane. "Then one day he was gone and when I asked Father where he went, he told me that he'd gone away, but that he would be fine."

"Oh dear," said Louise. "Maybe you do remember Oliver."

"What happened to him?" demanded Jane.

"Well, he died, of course," said Louise.

"Old age," added Alice. "Goodness, he must've been about fifteen."

"So I did know Oliver," said Jane with satisfaction. She turned to Mark and Adam. "Those two are always remembering something that happened before I was born, but I got them this time."

"You certainly did," admitted Louise. "Now that you mention it, I do remember that Father was unsure about how much to tell you at the time. You were quite young and probably would not have really comprehended that Oliver had died."

"Maybe," agreed Jane, "but it was upsetting, even to my child's mind, that Oliver had simply *gone away*. I imagined that he had packed his little kitty bag and taken off down the street to live with some other family. I think I even blamed myself, as if I'd been nicer to him he might've stayed."

Everyone laughed—everyone except Adam. Without even finishing his dinner, he excused himself and left the table.

"Oh dear," said Alice after they heard him go upstairs, "I think we came too close to his feelings about his parents."

Jane sighed. "It's really hard to predict what will upset him. I thought cats were a safe topic. Well, we are making some progress. At least he said 'excuse me' this time."

Mark just rolled his eyes and sighed deeply, then said, "My most sincere apologies, ladies."

Chapter Fifteen

"Poor Mark," said Jane as she and Alice finished up in the kitchen. "I think this thing with Adam is making him old before his time."

"I know how he feels," admitted Alice. "Adam does that to me too."

"He's not very subtle, is he?"

"What do you mean?"

"I mean he is so obviously ignoring you, Alice. It's almost humorous."

Alice hung up the dishtowel. "I guess I missed the funny part."

"Mark didn't want dessert?" asked Louise as she joined them.

"No," said Alice. "He said he just wanted to turn in early. Sounds like he and Adam are planning another full day tomorrow."

"Maybe it will help," said Louise as she put on the kettle. "At least it will keep him away from Laura." She lowered her voice. "I'm certain the Winstons will appreciate that."

"Are they back?" asked Alice.

"They just came in."

"I wonder if they'd like some dessert?" suggested Jane. "There's plenty of cherry cheesecake. I already offered some to the Langleys. I told them I'd set it up in the dining room and it would be self-serve."

"I'll go and ask them," offered Alice.

"Yes, and perhaps I will play for a bit," said Louise as she stretched her fingers. "I could use a little practice."

Alice found the Winstons still in the foyer, discussing whether they would turn in for the night. "Jane has made a lovely dessert," she told them. "Cherry cheesecake. We're setting it up in the dining room. If you'd care for any, just help yourselves. And Louise is going to play the piano tonight."

"Oh, that sounds wonderful," said Mrs. Winston.

Mr. Winston looked at his watch. "Not for me, thanks. I've got a good book I'd like to finish."

Laura just yawned and looked bored.

"Well, as always," said Alice, "just make yourselves at home." Then she returned to the kitchen.

Before long, the Langleys, Mrs. Winston, Laura and the three sisters were all settled into the parlor with dessert and tea. Louise began playing. Laura was seated by herself near the door, and Alice was not surprised when the teen, unnoticed by her mother, made a getaway. Alice had to give Laura credit; she was doing much better at finding her way around than when she had first arrived. Alice waited a couple of minutes, then carefully picked up a few of the empty dishes and made a quiet exit too. She was curious about where Laura had gone but did not see her in the foyer or on the stairs. After depositing the dishes in the dishwasher, Alice went out to the reception desk and paused to tidy up the paperwork and brochures there. It was then she heard quiet voices coming from behind the closed door to the library. She did not intend to eavesdrop, but Louise had stopped playing and the conversation in the library carried quite clearly to where Alice was working.

"He's so soft," cooed Laura.

"His name is Boots, because he's black with four white feet," said Adam. "Do you think that's lame? I mean like Puss in Boots."

"Oh, that sounds so cute. No, seriously, I think Boots is a cool name."

"Can you feel how skinny he is?"

"Yeah, he seems really bony."

"I think he was starving. He's not very old. Mark said he was probably too young to be weaned. I think maybe the mother cat died and he was left on his own."

"Kind of like you?"

"Yeah, I guess, sort of."

Then Louise began playing again, and the rest of their conversation was lost in the music. Still, what little she heard made her heart soften toward Adam. She suspected that Adam's hard veneer was just a protective coating that kept him from getting hurt. Alice couldn't understand why he was so wary of her. She had no intention of hurting the boy. Of course, he could not know that. Goodness, he barely knew her. She would just have to be very patient.

She returned to the parlor and stood by the door. Jane was comfortably seated in an easy chair, flipping through a magazine as she listened to Louise. Mrs. Winston was sitting next to Mrs. Langley, and both women were leaning back into the sofa with closed eyes, as if the calming music was transporting them to another time and place. Alice felt sure that Mrs. Winston had yet to notice her daughter's absence, and Alice did not feel the need to inform her. Mrs. Winston looked so peaceful and relaxed, and Laura was perfectly fine and just a few feet away down the hallway.

Without being observed, Alice went back out of the room and then upstairs. It was not that she was physically tired, but she was weary of all the comings and goings. On top of that, there was Adam and his strong dislike of her. Alice thought that was enough to make anyone weary.

She picked up the quilt but set it aside almost immediately. She had made good progress on it earlier today, and to work on it at night, when she was not her clearest, might be inviting trouble. Alice detested picking apart seams. She took off her shoes and put on slippers, then picked up her mystery book. She was about halfway through it. Although it was not her favorite type of mystery, it had finally gotten her hooked. She wondered what had become of the missing curator of the museum, kind old Mr. Beacon with the wooden leg. She hoped that he was all right. He didn't deserve to come to harm.

It was after ten o'clock when Alice paused in her reading. Her eyes were getting blurry and she knew she should go to bed. Oddly enough, she did not feel the least bit sleepy. It must be a cocoa night, she told herself, as she slipped out of her room and quietly began down the stairs. All was silent in the house now. She was careful on the fifth stair down since she knew it had a squeak in it. She hurried past the second floor and on down into the darkened kitchen, and before long her cocoa was nice and hot. She turned off the lights in the kitchen, then moved toward the stairs. A sliver of light coming from under the door to the library stopped her. *Had Adam and Laura forgotten to turn off the light?* she wondered. Of course, it wasn't a big deal, but living all those years with her father had taught her to be conservative when it came to electricity—especially about turning off lights. So she walked over to the library. She was just reaching for the knob when she heard voices again. Adam and Laura. Now this surprised Alice.

"*Pssst*," came a quiet whisper from the parlor.

Alice tiptoed down the hallway to the darkened parlor.

"It's Steph Winston, Alice," whispered a woman's voice.

"Mrs. Winston?" Alice whispered back. She paused in the doorway, her eyes slowly adjusting to the darkness until she saw a figure sitting in the easy chair.

"Yes. I'm being something of a chaperone," she explained. "Or perhaps an overprotective and snoopy mother."

Alice smiled. "I understand completely."

"I hadn't really meant to listen," she admitted, "but when I did it was oddly reassuring."

"I know what you mean." Alice partially closed the door. Just in case. "I overheard a bit of their conversation earlier this evening."

"As crazy as it sounds, I'm beginning to think that boy is good medicine for my daughter."

"I had the same thought. In fact, I think maybe your daughter is good medicine for Adam too."

"They are both rather needy."

"I know," said Alice, "and they seem to understand each other."

"Perhaps it's one of those blessings in disguise," said Mrs. Winston.

"I think you are right."

"But even so . . . well, I just feel a little uneasy about leaving them down here all alone."

"I don't blame you."

"I certainly don't want him taking her off in the middle of the night," said Mrs. Winston. "But I'm getting very sleepy."

Alice sat down in the chair by the door, careful not to spill her cocoa. "How about if I take over for you?"

"Oh, I couldn't—"

"No, it's all right," said Alice. "I came down because I couldn't sleep anyway. If they carry on for too long, I'll simply play housemother and tell them it's time to call it a night."

"Oh, that would be so much better coming from you," said Mrs. Winston gratefully.

"I think so too."

Mrs. Winston stood. "Well, thank you then. I really do appreciate it."

"I'll make sure they wrap it up by eleven," said Alice.

After Mrs. Winston left, Alice leaned back into the chair and sipped cocoa. Although she wasn't trying to, she could hear the voices of the two young people next door.

"You can't give up," Adam was saying. "I mean, look at you, Laura. You've got everything going for you."

"Like what?"

"You're smart and pretty, you've got both your parents, and they really seem to care about you."

"They suffocate me."

"They love you, Laura."

"Yeah, I guess."

"You know what I would give to have my parents back?"

Now there was a long silence.

"No, what?"

"Everything."

"I'm sorry, Adam."

"I wasn't trying to hold a pity party," he said quickly. "I just wanted to remind you that you're lucky. In fact, I would gladly give up my eyesight if it would bring my parents back."

"Yeah, I know . . ."

"And I'm not trying to make it seem like it's no big deal, Laura. I mean I can't imagine what it feels like to be blind, but I think you can make things work for you. You can take those classes your parents keep pushing and—"

"Just give in to it, you mean?"

"It's not like you have a choice, you know."

There was a long pause and Alice wondered what she should do. Were they finished talking now? Was it time for her to go in, play the chaperone and help them to call it a night?

"What about you, Adam?" said Laura finally. "Are *you* ever going to just give in to it?"

"What do you mean?"

"Well, look at you. I mean everyone can see it, even me and I'm blind."

Adam gave a little laugh. "What do you mean? What can you see?"

"That you're pushing everyone away from you. I mean the ones who probably care the most anyway. Like Dr. Graves and, well, Alice too. My mom says it's because they're a couple and that it probably bugs you or something."

"That's not it. I don't care if they're a couple or not. What difference does it make to me anyway?"

"So then why are you so mean to her?"

"I don't know . . ."

"She's really nice, Adam. You should get to know her."

"Why?" he said in a louder voice. "Why should I bother? I mean what if I do get to know her? And even Mark too?

What difference does it make if they're just going to leave me anyway?"

"You don't know that."

"Everybody leaves," he said in a bitter voice. "Even my grandma is talking about going into a home now. I know she's old and everything, and she can't stick around forever. Everyone just leaves eventually—" his voice broke.

"You don't know that, Adam."

"It's how life is," he said. "Even if it's all wrong. It's the way things are, you know."

"Things can change," she told him.

"Yeah, they can get worse. It's just not fair."

Alice could hear Adam crying now. She could also hear Laura trying to say things to comfort him—quiet, soothing things. It was sweet, but Alice suspected, by his response, that he was feeling embarrassed. It sounded as if he was trying to push Laura away.

"It's no big deal," he said in a gruff voice. "I don't know why I even said all that stuff. Just forget about it, okay."

"But it's—"

"Look, it's really late, Laura. I'm sure your parents will be down here with a shotgun before long."

"No, that's okay—"

"It's late," he insisted. "Come on, let's get you upstairs before someone's down here reading me the riot act."

Just like that, without Alice having to play housemother or even say a word, the two young people took themselves upstairs, and soon the inn was completely quiet.

Alice wiped away a tear as she stood. More than ever, she felt sorry for Adam. So that was what he was doing—pushing people away to avoid being hurt. It was a wonder he was allowing Mark into his life. Even then it seemed like two steps forward and one step back, but at least it made some sense now.

She longed to tell Mark about what she had heard. She knew how discouraged he had been when he went to his room earlier this evening. She returned her empty cocoa cup to the kitchen sink, then tiptoed up the stairs, pausing at Mark's door. Dare she knock? If she did, how would it look? At least she was still in her daytime clothes. But still . . .

As much as she wanted to let Mark know what she had heard, she knew it would have to wait until morning. Besides, there was not any light coming from under his door. He was probably fast asleep. On the other hand, she could see light beneath Adam's door. She did not dare chance his overhearing her tell Mark that she had been eavesdropping on him and Laura. No, that would not do at all.

Alice continued on up to her room, knowing that this news had to keep until the morning. Before she went to sleep, she said a special prayer for Adam. She asked that God would somehow soften him, so that he might allow people back into his life. He was far too young to be trapped into a life of bitterness and seclusion. He needed to get rid of the bitterness before the bitterness took hold of him. Perhaps she would not be able to speak to him directly, but she could talk to Mark.

Even better than that, she could pray. *And pray*, she decided, *I will*.

Chapter Sixteen

"S o how goes it at the inn?" asked Vera when Alice showed up at the Humberts' house for their walk early the following morning.

"I'm feeling hopeful," said Alice. "As well as a little guilty."

"Guilty?"

"Well, for eavesdropping . . . sort of." Then she explained the bits of Adam and Laura's conversation that she had overheard last night.

"Oh, that's not exactly eavesdropping," said Vera. "That was more like chaperoning. You had promised Laura's mother to watch out for her. I don't think there's anything wrong with that."

"And at least it was a positive conversation. Mark had been so down on Adam last night. He was so discouraged that he even went to bed early. I felt bad for him."

"Did you tell him about the conversation?"

"Not yet. I was the only one up this morning. I'll tell him when I get back. It should make him feel better."

"Well, it can't be easy for Adam to feel as if he's alone in the world at such a young age. I just saw a news show about twenty-something kids and how so many of them feel so lost.

Even after they graduate from college they don't know where they fit into the world."

"That's too bad, but at least they have finished college. Adam keeps telling everyone he has no interest in continuing his education."

"Oh," said Vera with a frown. "As a teacher, I can't understand that attitude. Well, if anyone can talk sense into that boy, it'll be Mark."

"I hope so."

"Are we going too far?" asked Vera. "Are your feet okay?"

"I'm okay," said Alice.

They walked and chatted and before Alice knew it, they were back at the inn. "Wow, that seemed to go fast," she said.

Vera nodded. "I better run. I just remembered that it's my turn to take treats to the teachers' lounge today. I still have to stop by the bakery."

Alice waved to her friend and then walked toward the inn. "Hey there, Wendell," she said as the cat ambled up to her and rubbed himself against her legs. "Have you met the new kitten yet?" Wendell just purred in that self-satisfied way of his, and Alice obligingly bent down to pet him.

"You're a good old cat," she finally told him after giving him a nice long scratch on his head and chin. "But I need to get inside and help Jane."

Alice took a quick peek around the inn, hoping maybe to spy Mark and take a few moments to tell him about what she had heard, but he didn't seem to be around.

"Hello, there," said Mr. Langley as he looked up from where he was comfortably reading his newspaper in the parlor. "I felt so good this morning that I decided to get up early and take a little stroll. The wife's still in bed."

"Well, good for you and for her," said Alice. "Isn't it nice to be able to do as you please while you're on vacation?"

"It sure is."

Alice hurried upstairs for a quick shower before she went back down to help Jane. Although it was not even seven o'clock yet, she suspected that Mr. Langley was getting hungry.

"Hey, you," said Jane as Alice came into the kitchen. "You're early this morning."

"I'm not the only one," said Alice as she put on an apron. "Mr. Langley's out there reading the paper and I think he's hungry."

Jane handed Alice a nicely arranged platter of pastries. "Why don't you put this out there along with the coffee pot and invite him to get started."

"Here you go, Mr. Langley," said Alice as she set the items on the dining room table, "there's coffee and pastries and I'll be back in a minute with some juice."

When she returned with pitchers of orange and apple juice, Mr. Langley had already sat down at the table and was helping himself to a nice plump croissant. "You ladies are going to have me spoiled by the time I go home," he said with a smile. "Not to mention fattened up."

"At least you've been getting some exercise," she said as she set the pitchers down. "Did you have a nice walk?"

"I sure did. And, I almost forgot, I saw your friend Dr. Graves as I was leaving and he asked me to tell you that he and Adam were taking a day trip. He would've told you himself, but you were gone."

"A day trip?"

"He said he was going with Adam to pay his respects to the gravesites of the young man's parents."

She nodded. "I see."

"It's a sad thing to lose your family like that."

"Yes, I feel bad for Adam."

"Anyway, Dr. Graves wanted me to let you know so you wouldn't worry."

"Thank you," said Alice. "I appreciate it." Although she did appreciate it, she felt sad that she had missed the chance to talk to Mark. Perhaps it would work out better this way. Maybe Adam was getting to the place where he would be ready to confide in Mark in the same way he had confided in Laura.

"What are your plans today?" asked Jane as Alice helped her to clean up after breakfast.

"I'm going collecting."

"Collecting?"

Alice grinned. "The prizes for the Easter egg hunt. I sent out the letters to the local businesses about a month ago. Now it's time to go around and see if they are willing to help out."

Jane made a face. "Good luck."

"Yes, I'll probably need it."

"You can put me down for chocolates," said Jane as she rinsed a mixing bowl. "I thought I'd try making some cute decorated eggs that I saw in my cooking magazine. I'll make a batch for the inn and if they turn out well, I'll do more for the baskets. How many are you going to fill?"

"We're planning on ten," said Alice. "The ANGELs and I will put them together tomorrow night."

"I'm sure they'll think that great fun."

"I hope so. It all depends on what the businesses want to contribute."

"I hope it won't be a bunch of old, useless stuff like last year," teased Jane. "What kid wants a shoe horn in his prize basket?"

"Or a tea ball." Alice chuckled. "Well, I was very specific

about contributions this year. I said they must be child-friendly and I even gave them the age categories."

"Well, I can't wait to see what you get," said Jane.

Alice put on her walking shoes again. Just as she was about to head out the door, the phone rang, and she went to pick it up. It was Aunt Ethel asking for help moving her couch. Alice promised to come by later to help her, then she took a sturdy shopping bag and set out on her mission. She decided that she would start at the hardware store. She knew that she could count on Vera's husband Fred to come up with something nice.

"Howdy, Alice," he said as soon as she entered the store. Alice loved the familiar old smell of this store. More than a hundred years old, it was as if the old walls could tell stories of the days gone by. Some of the merchandise probably could too— Alice felt certain that some of these same items had been on the shelves when she was a child. "Hi, Fred." She smiled and stood at the counter. "I've come collecting for the Easter baskets."

He grinned. "I thought maybe that's what the bag was for. Well, you're in luck this year." He stooped down to get something from behind the counter. "I got in far more of these things than I thought I'd ordered." He stood up and placed an assortment of water guns in varying sizes and colors on the counter. "There's ten altogether."

"That's great!" Alice nodded. "I'm sure the children will be delighted with those."

"The parents may not be too thrilled."

Alice began loading them into her bag. "We won't worry about that, will we, Fred?"

He chuckled. "Kind of like being a grandparent."

"Right. You can spoil them and not worry about the results. Any idea what the weather will be like this weekend?" Fred was an amateur meteorologist.

He rubbed his chin. "Well, the news is predicting cloudy,

maybe even showers, but I think it'll be all cleared up by the weekend."

"I hope you're right." She put the last squirt gun in her bag. "Thanks so much, Fred. These are great prizes."

The General Store's contribution was not too generous, but at least packs of gum were better than nothing.

She crossed Chapel Road to Nine Lives Bookstore. After entering, she paused to pet one of the shop cats, then went up to the counter.

"Good morning, Alice," said Viola as she lowered her glasses and set aside a thick book.

Alice quickly explained the reason for her visit. "If you haven't got anything, I'll understand."

"Of course, I have something," said Viola with a twinkle in her eye. "I think you'll be impressed too." Then Viola reached down below her counter and pulled out a stack of picture books. "These are hot off the press, not only that, but they are signed by the author."

"Really?" Alice picked up a book for a closer look.

"These are wonderful. Thank you. They will be a great addition to the baskets," Alice said as she walked toward the exit.

Her next stop was down Berry Lane at Wilhelm Wood's Time for Tea. "Good morning, Wilhelm," she said in a cheerful voice.

"Hello, Alice. I've just brewed some of my new spring blend. Would you like to sample it?"

"Certainly," she told him, waiting as he poured her a small cup.

"It's a green tea," he said, "that I infused with a bit of peppermint."

She took a sip. "Oh, this is lovely. It's very refreshing. I bet it would be good iced too."

He nodded. "Yes, that's what I thought."

Alice picked up a box and set it on the counter. "I'd like this, and I'm also here to see if you'd like to contribute anything to the Easter egg hunt prizes. Did you get my letter?"

"Yes, and do I have something for you. You said there would be ten baskets, right?"

"That's correct."

He went into his backroom and returned with a small basket of what appeared to be tiny fabric teapots. She picked one up. "What is it?"

"Smell," he said.

She took a whiff and was surprised that it smelled faintly of roses.

"They're sachets," he explained, "filled with potpourri." He looked slightly embarrassed now. "Mother makes them. She wants me to carry them in here, but I'm not so sure. What do you think, Alice?"

She studied the small calico teapot trimmed with lace. "This is very sweet. I think someone who loves tea and teapots would like them very much."

Wilhelm smiled. "They are rather cute, aren't they? Sort of a novelty item. Perhaps I should keep a basket of them up by the register."

"Do you have more?"

"Do I have more?" He groaned. "I probably have a hundred by now. Mother just keeps making them."

Alice laughed. "Well, maybe this will be a way to introduce them to the community."

"Yes," he said. "Perhaps you're right."

"Thank you, Wilhelm. And thank your mother too."

"By the way, Alice . . ." Wilhelm had a curious expression on his face. "What's going on with you and the veterinarian? Clara Horn is going around town telling everyone that you two will be married by summer."

Alice tried to laugh. "Oh dear, I better straighten poor Clara out."

Wilhelm frowned. "So, it's not true?"

"Not in the least."

"Dr. Graves seems such a nice fellow."

"Oh yes, he's very nice, and we are good friends." Alice made a movement toward the door.

"But no wedding bells?"

"Not for me."

He shook his head. "Too bad."

Alice just smiled and exited. *Really*, she wondered, w*hy would he think it was too bad?* Wilhelm himself was not married and, as far as Alice knew, he did not intend to marry anytime soon. While there were several single women who bought far more tea than they could use, Wilhelm did not seem to think of them as anything other than customers. It seemed to Alice that people always wanted someone else to get married. Maybe it was simply for the festivity of a wedding, or something to talk about, or perhaps some people assumed that one could not be happy without the blessed bonds of matrimony.

Alice sighed as she walked back over to Hill Street. The Good Apple bakery donated ten gaily wrapped giant cookies. "What kid doesn't like a cookie?" said Clarissa with a bright smile.

"You're right," said Alice as she slipped them, one by one, into her bag. "Thank you."

Next Alice went to Nellie's Dress Shop. After she greeted Nellie Carter, she felt somewhat apologetic. "I'll understand if you don't have anything to contribute," Alice told her. "I mean a dress shop —"

"Not at all," said Nellie. "I think I might have something rather fun. Well, at least I think the girls will like them. Maybe the boys can give them to their sisters or mothers." She laid some pairs of brightly colored socks on the counter. "See," she said, "some have Scotty dogs, others have cats, this pair has pigs, and there's even a pair with pink elephants."

"Those are fun," said Alice. "Thank you so much!"

Alice was not too sure about Sylvia's Buttons, the local fabric shop, but since she had sent a letter, she knew she should stop by. "Hi, Sylvia," she called.

"Alice," said Sylvia Songer. "How is the quilt coming?"

"Not as quickly as I hoped."

"Well, you've still got plenty of time before the baby shower."

"I hope so. Easter season is a bit distracting."

Sylvia smiled. "And then, of course, you've got the distraction of Dr. Graves as well . . ."

Alice shrugged. "Oh, that's not so distracting."

"That's not what I hear."

"I'm guessing you've been talking to Jane."

Sylvia leaned forward on the counter. "That Jane has hardly told me a thing. You'd think she'd been sworn to secrecy or something."

Alice laughed. "Well, it's only because there's nothing to tell."

"That's not what the rest of town is saying."

Alice decided not to bite.

Sylvia's eyebrows went up. "Don't you want to know?"

"I can guess."

"Well, your dear aunt has been dropping hints all over the place."

"No one takes Aunt Ethel too seriously."

"Let's just say there's plenty of speculation." Sylvia looked disappointed now. "So, you're really not going to tell me anything."

Alice sighed. "As I said, there's really nothing to tell." Then she forced a smile to her lips. "Now, I'm here on a mission, Sylvia. I know you may not have anything to contribute, but did you get my letter about the Easter egg hunt prizes?"

"I did and I do. I think you'll be pleased. I'll be right back."

While she waited, Alice looked through a pile of new fabric. Then Sylvia returned with all sorts of soft-looking fuzzy critters in her arms.

"They may be a bit young for some of the kids, but aren't they cute?" said Sylvia as she spread them over the counter.

"They're adorable." Alice picked up a soft blue bear.

"I taught a class on recycling chenille bedspreads and I gave the ladies a nice discount on everything in my shop if they agreed to sew and contribute one item for the Easter basket prize."

"Oh, Sylvia, you're a genius. These are wonderful."

"Aren't they!"

As Sylvia loaded the stuffed toys into another bag, since Alice's shopping bag was already rather full, Alice spoke in a lowered voice. "Now, if things should ever change between Mark and me, I promise to give Jane special permission to let you know."

Sylvia smiled. "Why, thank you, Alice."

"Thank you!"

Alice felt as if she had struck it rich in town today. Perhaps it had been a good idea to send out that letter of explanation beforehand after all. Her ANGELs would be thrilled with all the goodies to put in the baskets tomorrow night. These baskets would be so much better than last year.

Chapter  Seventeen

O h, Mark called," said Jane that evening as she sifted
flour into a large mixing bowl. "He and Adam aren't
going to be home in time for dinner tonight. He sends his
most sincere apologies."

"How did he sound?" asked Alice. "Could you tell how it
was going?"

"Well, to be honest, he sounded a little stressed to me. I
think he was disappointed that he wasn't able to speak to you."

Alice started to prepare a salad. "Yes, I wish I'd been
here. What time did he call?"

"It was while you were helping Aunt Ethel move her
couch. Maybe I should've come over and gotten you."

"That's okay," said Alice. "Although I would've appreciated a rescue."

"Where did she want it moved to anyway?" asked Jane.

Alice laughed. "Good question. First, she wanted it moved
over by the window, but it didn't fit quite right. Then she
wanted it in the center of the room, sort of like a room divider."

"In that tiny room?" Jane shook her head.

"Exactly," said Alice. "It looked odd."

"So where did you finally move it?"

"Right back to where it was in the first place."

"Well!"

Alice nodded. "My reaction exactly."

"I should've gone over to help," said Jane. "I would've simply told her that there was only one place for her couch and that's where it already was."

"Oh, I think she probably knows that already. She just enjoys rearranging things every once in a while." Alice transferred the lettuce that she had washed and spun dry into the wooden salad bowl. "Did Mark say anything about their visit to the cemetery?"

"Just that Adam was supposed to be giving the directions and that they got lost a few times. Adam didn't seem to remember where it was. Even when they found the memorial park, it took forever to find the right section."

"That must have been frustrating."

"That Adam," said Jane as she cracked an egg. "He seems to frustrate people even when he's not trying to."

Alice told Jane a bit of the conversation that she had overheard last night. "I know it wasn't much," she said, "but it did give me hope, and I wanted to tell Mark about it."

"Speaking of Adam," said Jane, "I wonder how that poor kitten is doing. Do you think he left it here?"

"Goodness, I don't know," said Alice. "Should I check his room just in case?"

"I think so. That poor creature could be up there starving for all we know. Didn't Mark say it needed to eat every few hours?"

Alice nodded as she set down her knife and wiped her hands. She went to the office, grabbed up the keys and hurried to the second floor. She did not like intruding on Adam's space, but the sisters did go into guest rooms to replace linens and whatnot. As usual, she tapped on the door, although she knew no one was there, then she unlocked the door and let herself in. She was surprised to see that Adam was actually keeping things rather neat.

She glanced around the room, looking for the cat carrier that Mark had bought, but she didn't see it anywhere. Finally, satisfied that the kitten was not there and, consequently not suffering, she started to leave. But something stopped her. She noticed that a Bible, one of the ones that Louise had placed in each room, was sitting on the nightstand, opened up as if Adam had been reading it. Well, that was something, after all.

She quietly closed the door and locked it.

"Who's that?" said a voice.

Alice jumped and turned around to see Laura standing in the open doorway to the guest room she was sharing with her parents.

"Oh," said Alice. "It's just me, Alice. Goodness, you startled me. I didn't realize anyone was up here."

"Why were you in Adam's room?" Laura adjusted her sunglasses in such a way that Alice almost felt that the young woman was studying her, although she knew that couldn't be.

"Well, I just learned that Mark and Adam have been delayed and won't be back until late. Jane and I were worried about Adam's kitten. We thought that poor Boots might be stuck up here without—"

"Adam asked me to watch Boots for him today."

"Oh good. That's a relief. How's the little guy doing?"

Laura smiled. "I think he's okay. Do you want to come in here and check on him? I mean Adam showed me how to open the can of food, and how much to give him and stuff, but my parents have been gone, and, well, I just hope I haven't done anything wrong, you know."

"I'd be happy to check on him, but I'm sure he's all right."

Alice followed Laura into the room, watching as Laura felt her way around the bedroom furnishings. "You're getting around much better, Laura."

"Yeah," said Laura when she made it to the roll-away cot and sat down. She leaned over and reached for the cat crate that was right beside it. "I guess I'm trying a little harder."

Alice watched as Laura opened the latch on the cat crate and then carefully extracted the small black and white kitten. She held the kitten up and Alice reached out and caressed its soft head. "He looks perfectly fine to me, Laura."

"I'm trying not to handle him too much," she said. "My mom told me that kittens could get sick if you hold them too much."

"He looks perfectly fine and happy too."

Laura smiled as she held the kitten against her cheek. "That's what I thought, but I wasn't sure."

"Sometimes I think we can tell things better with our hands than with our eyes," said Alice. "For instance, I sometimes work in the neonatal nursery at the hospital, when they're shorthanded, and I've discovered that I can tell as much, and more, by the way a baby feels, breathes and sounds as I can by simply looking at it."

Laura nodded. "Yeah, I guess that kinda makes sense."

"In fact, I think we can be deceived sometimes when we rely only on our eyes. It's as if God gave us these other senses to help us to understand life better, but often we forget to develop them fully."

"You mean until we're forced to?"

"Maybe so."

Laura bent over and put the kitten back into the carrier, gently pushing it back so that she could safely close and then latch the door. "Thanks, Alice," she said as she sat back up.

"You're welcome. I can see that Boots is in very good hands. I'm sure that Adam will be pleased when he gets back."

"Do you know when that'll be?"

"I don't know. It sounds as if they have a long drive ahead."

Laura nodded. "It must be really sad."

"What's that?" asked Alice, although she thought she knew.

"I mean for Adam, being all alone like that, and then going to see his parents' graves today. Well, it just seems really sad."

"Adam's not completely alone," said Alice. "At least he has Mark."

"I don't know if Adam really believes that, I mean deep down, you know."

Alice sighed. "Well, maybe we can all try to help him to understand that there are other people who care for him, people who want to help."

"Yeah, I told him he shouldn't be pushing people away."

"That's good advice, Laura."

"I'm not sure that it did any good though."

"Sometimes it takes awhile for things to sink in. Maybe today's trip with Mark will help."

"I hope so."

"Hello," said Mrs. Winston from the hallway. She looked concerned as she removed her jacket. "Is everything okay in here?"

Alice smiled at her. "Yes, everything's fine. Laura was just letting me have a peek at Boots. She's done a wonderful job of kitty-sitting today."

Mr. Winston frowned. "She refused to go out with us this afternoon, said she had to take care of Adam's cat."

Mrs. Winston gently nudged her husband. "And that was just fine, dear."

"Well, do you think we could talk you into coming out for a bite of dinner now, Laura," he asked in a slightly irritated tone, "or will that be too much inconvenience for our fine furry friend?"

Alice laughed. "Oh, I'm sure Boots will be just fine. In fact, I'll be happy to watch him while you're gone."

Alice suspected that Laura would have preferred staying in and caring for the kitten, but her parents seemed relieved that she agreed to join them for dinner in Potterston.

Alice took the crate downstairs and, with Jane's permission, placed it in a quiet corner in the kitchen and got Boots all settled.

Then the three sisters sat down to a quiet dinner.

"How did your prize collection for the Easter egg hunt go today?" Louise asked Alice.

"Quite well." Then she told about some of the pleasant surprises.

"Speaking of Easter, is Cynthia going to make it here for the holiday?" asked Alice.

"She was unsure when I spoke with her, but that was several days ago. Perhaps things will change by the weekend."

"Maybe I'll have to e-mail that niece of mine," said Jane. "Perhaps toss a little guilt into the message. See if that doesn't make her think twice."

Louise chuckled. "That would be much better coming from an aunt than a mother."

"Speaking of aunts," said Jane. "I heard from Craig Tracy that our dear aunt is telling townsfolk that one of her nieces is hearing wedding bells these days." She looked directly at Alice now.

Alice frowned. "Yes, I heard that in town today too."

"Well, I am sure that people were already making their own assumptions anyway," said Louise. "We can't blame it all on Aunt Ethel."

"I actually tried to set Auntie straight today," said Alice as she buttered a slice of sourdough bread. "When we were, uh, moving furniture."

"Poor Alice," said Jane. She explained to Louise about their aunt's desire to rearrange the carriage house. "This week is supposed to be a vacation for you, but it seems you've been busier than ever."

Alice smiled. "I guess I'll be glad to go back to work next week."

"But what about *this thing*?" asked Louise.

Alice blinked. "What thing?"

"This thing with Mark, of course."

"There is no *thing* with Mark, Louise." Alice looked directly into her older sister's pale blue eyes. "Honestly, if there was a thing, I would tell you. You must know that."

"They haven't even had time to have a thing," added Jane with a twinkle in her eye. "Mark's got his hands full with his young man."

Louise and Jane began discussing Adam. Alice threw in some words in his defense, but finally she just gave up and started clearing the table. Their observations about Adam were not untrue, but it made her uncomfortable to hear them just the same.

"Oh dear," said Louise as she looked at the clock. "I almost forgot that the book group meets tonight. I promised Viola that I would be there early."

"And I'm going to Sylvia's," said Jane. "She invited me over to watch a video with her tonight." Jane looked at Alice. "You're welcome to join us if you like."

"No, thanks," she said as she rinsed a plate. "Why don't you let me finish cleaning things up in here, and you two go ahead and take off."

"Oh, I don't want to leave you with—"

"I insist," said Alice firmly. "I think I'll turn in early tonight, or perhaps I'll work on the baby quilt a bit."

Alice, with the company of the kitten, finished putting things back in order in the kitchen. Just as she finished up, she heard the sound of the Winstons' voices as they returned from dinner.

Alice gave Boots back to Laura and then told them good night. Once in her room, Alice wondered about Mark and Adam. She imagined them driving back toward Acorn Hill in the dark, perhaps having a nice conversation. Maybe Adam was actually opening up to Mark. She could only pray that was happening.

She tried not to think about Louise's questions about her and Mark. Certainly there was nothing to report. Alice was not sure if that was because of her, or Adam, or Mark.

She wondered if things would have gone differently if Adam had not come to the inn. To be perfectly honest, she was not even sure how she would prefer to have had things go. Oh, she did enjoy Mark's friendship, and she was fond of him.

What good does it do to dwell on such things anyway? she thought. She pushed these thoughts from her mind. Then, thankful for the distraction, she focused all her attention into the careful construction of a quilt block.

Chapter  Eighteen

A lice surprised herself by sewing late into the evening and consequently sleeping in later than usual. She got out of bed, hurriedly dressed and practically jogged over to Vera's house. She noticed the gathering of clouds overhead and hoped that Fred's forecast for the bad weather to come and go before Easter was correct.

"I'm sorry I'm late," she called breathlessly when she saw Vera waiting on her front step. "Maybe we can make this a quick walk."

"It's all right," said Vera as she joined her. "Is everything okay?"

"Of course." Alice told her that it was the baby quilt project that had kept her up late. "I can't believe how late I stayed up working on it."

Vera smiled. "So you and Mark obviously didn't have a date?"

Alice shook her head. "He and Adam must have arrived home very late last night. They left early yesterday to visit Adam's parents' graves."

"So you didn't get a chance to talk to him then?"

"No, but I hope to today. I'm praying that things have begun turning around for Adam," she said.

After their walk, Alice and Vera parted and Alice went home to shower and dress. She knew that she was dressing more carefully than usual, and she admitted to herself that she was hoping to spend some time with Mark that day. As a result, she felt a mixture of nervousness and anticipation.

It was relatively quiet when she went downstairs to join Jane in the kitchen. She was surprised to see Louise already there, washing and stemming strawberries for a fruit platter.

"You're up early," she said to Louise.

"Or perhaps you are late," suggested Louise.

Alice looked at the clock. "I guess you're right. Need any help?"

"Everything's under control," said Jane. "But you could set up the coffee and tea. Is anyone up yet?"

"I didn't see a soul," said Alice as she carried the coffee and tea things out to the dining room.

"Good morning," said Mrs. Winston, coming into the dining room with her husband and Laura trailing behind.

"Good morning," said Alice. "It looks like our weather is changing today."

"I noticed that," said Mrs. Winston as she waited to take Laura's arm to guide her to the table.

Soon the others were coming in, and before long the dining room was nearly full. Mark and Alice exchanged greetings and she inquired about his trip the day before.

"A lot of driving," said Mark, glancing uneasily at Adam, who looked as sulky as ever, "but I'm glad I went."

Adam's eyes darted toward Mark, then back down as he silently sipped a cup of coffee.

The guests chatted congenially about things like the

weather and some recent news events and, before long, they began finishing their breakfasts and leaving, until only Adam and Mark remained at the table. Jane and Louise had quietly slipped off to the kitchen, but not without first eyeing Alice as if to warn her she was not to budge.

Alice suspected that Mark wanted to talk to her. She knew she definitely wanted to talk to him, if only to encourage him about Adam and to relate the hopeful things she had overheard.

Mark set down his coffee cup and cleared his throat. "Adam noticed a place over in Potterston," he began. "It's a recreation center that has a rock climbing wall."

"Oh yes," said Alice. "I've seen that place. It's new and I've heard it's quite nice."

Mark nodded. "I told him I'd take him over to check it out today."

"That's a good idea." Alice used a positive tone that she hoped covered up her disappointment. "It's a perfect thing to do on a rainy day."

Adam looked curiously at her.

"Would you like to join us?" asked Mark with a smile.

Alice could not tell if that was a genuine invitation or if Mark was simply being polite. She did know that she had absolutely no interest in rock climbing and even less interest in tagging along on this kind of adventure with Adam and Mark. "No, thank you," she said with a smile. "I'm sure you two will have a good time."

"Adam's dad was a rock climber."

"Really?" She glanced at Adam now. "Did you ever get to climb with him?"

He shrugged. "Not much. He mostly did it when he was younger, but he kept promising to teach me . . . someday."

She turned back to Mark. "How about you?" she asked with a bit of concern. "Have you done it before?"

"Oh yeah. Gregory and I climbed occasionally in high school. We did a couple of great trips back then. Of course, that was long before Adam was born. Gregory was actually a lot better at it than I was, but I always had fun. It's a good challenge to stretch yourself."

She sort of laughed. "I think that's more stretching than I would enjoy."

"Well, I'm guessing we'll be back around noon." He smiled at her. "Then perhaps you and I could do something together?"

"That would be nice," she told him.

He looked relieved and she wondered if he had been worried that she would be offended or hurt by his choice to do something with Adam rather than with her. Surely, he did not think she was that childish. Of course, Mark had been spending a lot of time with a young adult lately, and she hoped that he was not getting her confused with him.

"I hope you both have a wonderful time," she told them as she cleared the last of the breakfast things from the table. "I'll look forward to seeing you this afternoon, Mark."

Alice carried the cups and plates into the kitchen where Jane was loading the dishwasher.

"How'd that go?" asked Jane.

"What do you mean?" Alice rinsed the dishes and handed them to her sister.

"You know," Jane persisted, "with you and Mark and Adam."

"There wasn't much to it really."

Alice paused as Louise and Ethel came in the back door.

"Oh, it's starting to rain cats and dogs out there," said

Ethel as she removed her cardigan and gave it a shake. She patted her hair back into place. "I wish I'd thought to grab my umbrella." She smiled at Jane and Alice. "Looks as if I might be stranded here until it lets up."

"Did you come to pick up the truffles for Lloyd?" asked Jane as she set a box on the counter. "They're all ready."

"Yes," said Ethel. "He needs them for his city council meeting at noon."

"Is this some sort of bribe?" asked Jane.

Ethel laughed. "Of course not. Do you think our honorable mayor would resort to such tactics?"

"Well, I heard that the council is giving him a hard time about his proposal to put that four-way stop in."

Ethel waved her hand. "Oh, pish-posh, this is simply Lloyd's little Easter treat for the council."

"Is he going to wear his Easter bunny outfit for the meeting?" asked Jane with a teasing smile.

Ethel firmly shook her head. "No, and for your information, it's a *Mr. Easter Rabbit* suit, and Lloyd only wears it for the Easter egg hunt." She turned to Alice now. "Are we all set for that?"

"Well, other than the egg-dyeing party on Friday. I've collected the prizes and the ANGELs will put together the baskets tonight."

"The order of candy eggs arrived last week," said Louise.

"And I'll be boiling all the real eggs tomorrow," said Jane.

Ethel clapped her hands. "Thank goodness we're all so efficient. Now, how about giving your auntie a cup of coffee?"

Louise nudged Alice as Jane and Ethel headed for the coffee maker. "How did it go with Mark?" she asked in a lowered voice.

Alice shrugged. "Fine."

Ethel turned and looked at them. "Are you talking about your veterinarian, Alice?"

"You can call him Mark, Aunt Ethel."

"Of course, dear. How is it going?"

Alice was getting a bit weary of the inquisition. She felt silly since there was nothing new on this topic. "Mark is doing just fine," she told all three of them. "He and Adam have gone rock climbing this morning."

"Rock climbing?" Louise's eyes grew large. "In this sort of weather?"

"My goodness," said Ethel. "Are those two trying to kill themselves?"

Jane frowned. "That does seem a bit foolish, Alice."

Alice sighed. "They are doing indoor rock-climbing."

"What on earth are you talking about?" demanded Ethel.

Jane's eyes lit up. "Oh, I'll bet I know. They went over to the new recreation center in Potterston."

Alice simply nodded.

Jane explained the concept of an indoor rock-climbing wall to Ethel and Louise. "It's really fun," she finished up. "I did it a few times back in San Francisco. I wish I'd known they were going. I might've tagged along."

"I'm sure they would've enjoyed your company," said Alice.

Jane laughed. "I'm sure they would not. Adam probably would've thrown a fit."

For whatever reason, Alice found that she was tired of speculating over both Mark and Adam. "If you ladies will excuse me," she said, "I thought I might use this free morning to work on the baby quilt."

"Of course," said Ethel. "How's it coming anyway?"

Alice smiled. "It's looking more and more like a quilt."

"It's turning out to be very lovely," said Jane.

"Happy sewing," called Louise as Alice left the kitchen.

Alice paused in the living room to look out the window at the wet and blustery day. Gray and dark, it really was the perfect sort of day to cloister oneself in one's own room and get lost in a quilting project.

Chapter  Nineteen

It was nearly one in the afternoon when Alice emerged from her room. She hurried downstairs, worried that perhaps she was keeping Mark waiting.

Mr. and Mrs. Langley greeted her in the foyer. "We're just heading out for a bit of lunch," said Mr. Langley with a bright smile. "Would you like to join us, Alice?"

"Thank you," she told him, "but I already have plans."

"With Dr. Graves?" asked Mrs. Langley with friendly interest.

Alice nodded. "Yes, I was just looking for him."

"I haven't seen him come back," said Mr. Langley. "I've been sitting down here reading the paper for nearly an hour."

"Oh, then I'm sure he'll be here any minute," said Alice with confidence.

"Looks as if the rain's let up some," said Mrs. Langley. "Perhaps we should get going while the going's good."

Alice wished them a pleasant lunch, then went off in search of her sisters. She found Louise dusting in the parlor. "Have you seen Mark?" she asked.

"Not since breakfast." Louise set the pastel-toned porcelain figure of a shepherd girl back on the shelf and turned to Alice. "How is the quilt coming?"

"Nicely," said Alice. "It's such a comforting sort of project, sewing pieces neatly together and making everything line up just so."

"A bit like a jigsaw puzzle."

"Something like that. Nice and neat and orderly." Alice chuckled. "I guess I'm a fussbudget at heart."

"You simply enjoy order," said Louise as she dusted a cloisonné vase. "Nothing wrong with that."

Alice glanced at her watch. "I think I'll ask Jane if she has seen or heard from Mark."

She found Jane in the kitchen, bent over a recipe book wearing a slight scowl. "Is there something the matter?" she asked her younger sister.

Jane looked up. "Oh, I'm fine. I just don't understand this recipe. It somehow doesn't seem right, and I can't find my regular recipe."

Alice laughed. "Well, knowing you, Jane, you'll have created a completely new recipe by the time you're done."

Jane nodded. "That's probably just what I should do." Then she looked up from the book. "Hey, I thought you had a date with Mark this afternoon?"

"Well, it wasn't a date exactly, but I thought we were supposed to be getting together." Alice looked at the kitchen clock, which read one-thirty now. "Maybe I misunderstood. You haven't seen or heard from him, have you?"

"Nope, and I've been in the house all morning. So has Louise."

"I'm sure he and Adam must've just forgotten the time," said Alice. "Perhaps they ran late and decided to stop for lunch."

Jane closed the book and folded her arms across her chest. "Well, that's just wrong, Alice. If Mark keeps this up I will have a hard time liking that man."

"Oh, I'm sure it's—"

"Really, Alice. He can't keep asking you to play second fiddle to that boy. If Mark has feelings for you, he should come right out with it and—"

"Oh, I don't expect him to do that. I just thought it might be nice to have a quiet talk with him. That's all."

Jane rolled her eyes. "Oh, please, Alice. You know that's not all. You've been walking around here on needles and pins ever since Mark arrived. Don't act as if it's no big deal."

"But . . ." Alice stopped, then said slowly, "actually, I'm not sure what it is, Jane."

"What do you want it to be?"

"I'm not sure about that either."

Jane stepped closer, looking into Alice's eyes as if she could see deeper, as if she somehow knew what Alice herself did not know.

Alice grew uncomfortable, blinked and stepped back.

"Come on, Alice," urged Jane. "How do you really feel about him?"

Alice did not want to be dishonest with her sister. "The truth is I'm not sure."

"Not sure?"

Alice nodded.

"Okay, I'll quit pestering you, dear sister." Jane reached out and hugged Alice. "I just don't like seeing you going around with this cloud hanging over you. It's so unlike you."

"Really?" said Alice with interest. "Does it seem to you that I've had a cloud hanging over me?"

Jane nodded. "I've just assumed it's because you are trying to sort things out with Mark, and with Adam too. I'm sure it's been frustrating, but I'm so used to you as a cheerful, stable, contented person. And lately, well, you haven't exactly been yourself."

"I know . . ." Alice sighed.

"Well, I'm sure that everything will fall into place," said Jane.

Alice was not so sure, but she knew that it was useless to keep talking about it. "I think I'll fix a bite of lunch," said Alice, heading toward the refrigerator. "Then perhaps I'll go back to my quilt project. Would you like something?"

"No, thanks. Louise and I already ate."

Alice made a turkey sandwich, which she took back to her room with her. She didn't want to seem unsociable, but she also didn't want to be questioned by her sisters or by her aunt, if she popped in again. Although they had plenty of questions, Alice had no answers.

Alice decided to put Mark out of her mind after she finished her lunch and returned to her sewing. Surely, he and Adam were just fine. Perhaps today was the day when Mark would have that breakthrough with Adam. Wasn't that what she had been praying for? To sit around feeling sorry for herself was not only silly, it was also a waste of time.

It was nearly four o'clock when Jane came upstairs to tell Alice that she had a phone call. "It's someone from your work," said Jane. "If they want you to come in, you better say no."

Alice hurried down to get the phone.

"This is Alice."

"This is Peggy from ER."

"What's up, Peggy?"

"Well, I have a friend of yours here," said Peggy.

"A friend?" Alice felt a chill of alarm run through her. "Who?"

"He's a guest from your inn," said Peggy. "Mark Graves."

"What's wrong?" Alice's heart began to pound.

"It's not serious, Alice. Apparently he and his young friend were climbing a rock wall here in Potterston and Mark slipped and broke his arm."

"Oh dear."

"Yes, it was a nasty break. He's in surgery with Dr. Tyler right now."

Alice sighed. "At least he's in good hands."

"That's for sure."

"Is there anything I can do?"

"No, he just wanted you to know."

"When will they release him?"

"If all goes well, he should be out by this evening."

"Should I come to pick him up?"

"No, he specifically said to tell you not to worry about that. He said his young friend will drive him back to the inn and that he'll see you later."

"Well, thank you," said Alice. "Do tell him that I'm thinking of him and I hope that he's feeling better after surgery."

"I'm sure he will be."

"Please feel free to call, Peggy, if I can be of any help."

"Of course. By the way, how's your little vacation?"

When Alice heard the word "vacation," she almost laughed. "It's been interesting. Thanks again for calling, Peggy."

"No problem."

After Alice hung up, she told Jane about the bad news.

"Oh, poor Mark," said Jane.

"What happened to Mark?" said Louise as she came down the stairs.

Alice related the story to Louise.

"Goodness, what a bit of bad luck." Louise shook her head.

"I'm beginning to think that *Adam* is a bit of bad luck," said Jane.

"Oh, it's not his fault."

"Don't be so sure," said Jane quickly. "Adam keeps pushing Mark to do things—things that he may be a little too old to be doing."

"That is true," agreed Louise. "I think Adam is not only a bad influence on Laura, but on Mark as well."

"Speaking of Laura," said Jane, "how is she doing?"

"Her mother told me that she's been kitten-sitting again," said Louise. "Mrs. Winston was rather put out that Adam had not returned yet. I should go and tell her about Mark's accident. At least that gives Adam an excuse."

"It's not really Adam's fault," said Alice as Louise headed back up the stairs.

"Not directly," said Jane, "but think about it, Alice. Mark never would've broken his arm if Adam hadn't challenged him."

"I'm sure that Adam feels bad."

"Maybe." Jane made a sly face. "Or maybe Adam is like that movie from the fifties—*The Bad Seed*. Do you remember watching it on TV?"

"Oh, Jane." Alice just shook her head. "Adam is not a bad seed."

Jane laughed. "No, I don't think he is, but it does make you think."

"Perhaps it would be better to pray."

Jane nodded. "Yes, as usual, I'm sure you're right. Sorry I said that, Alice. It wasn't very nice."

"And, really," said Alice, "Adam can't be feeling too good right now."

"Serves him right." Then Jane winked at Alice and headed to the kitchen.

∞

Mark and Adam didn't get home in time for dinner or before it was time for Alice to head over to the Assembly Room in the chapel to set things up for the ANGELs meeting. Even with Jane helping, it took two trips to take the prizes, baskets and the evening's treats down to the basement room.

"Need any help?" offered Jane.

"I think we'll be fine," said Alice as she set down her last load. "Although you know that you're always more than welcome to join us."

"Thanks, but I think I'll start boiling those eggs," said Jane. "I think I can get about half of them done tonight."

"That sounds like a good idea."

Soon the girls began arriving and, as Alice had suspected, they began to ooh and aah over the prizes.

"These are way better than last year's prizes," said Jenny. "Way to go, Miss Howard."

"Yeah," agreed Ashley as she held up one of the chenille toys. "I wouldn't mind winning one of these baskets for myself."

"You're too old," said Sarah.

The ANGELs put the baskets together with very little help from Alice, laughing and joking as they worked.

"I think they should change the age limit from ten," said

Ashley. "I mean, just because we're older doesn't mean that we don't like to hunt for eggs."

"It wouldn't be fair," said Jenny. "The older kids would find all the eggs and then how would the little kids feel?"

"Besides," said Sarah, "Who would hide the eggs?"

"That's right," said Jenny. "That's lots more fun anyway."

"Don't forget," added Alice. "You're the ones who have to go around and look for all the missed eggs afterward."

"There were hardly any left over last year," said Ashley.

"Maybe we should hide them better," said Jenny. "Maybe if we started earlier we could come up with some better places."

"Yeah," said Ashley. "We could make it really hard."

"Not too hard," Alice said. "Remember some of the kids are barely able to toddle. You need some easy ones for them."

"They have their parents to help them," said Jenny. "Did you see how many eggs little Tommy Sanders got last year? His basket was so loaded that the handle actually broke."

"Yeah, my mom said that his dad should've been embarrassed for being so greedy."

Alice laughed. "Don't worry, there are plenty of eggs. Remember it's about having fun."

Soon the gift baskets were filled. The girls wrapped them in colorful cellophane that Jane had found at a craft store and carefully tied large pastel-colored ribbons into big bows on the tops of each one.

"These are beautiful, Miss Howard," said Ashley, her eyes glowing with pride. "Don't you think they're the best ones ever?"

Alice smiled as she recalled the prize baskets from when

she had been young. In her mind's eye, they had been even bigger and better than these, but she had been a little girl then. Things look very different when you're young. "You could be right, Ashley," she told her.

When they had finished with the baskets, they had their treat of homemade gingersnaps and punch. Then it was time to review the previous week's memory verses. Alice was pleased that all the ANGELs were well prepared, and she happily gave them prizes, in addition to the chocolate eggs that Jane had made for the girls.

"Wow," said Jenny, "double prizes tonight!"

"Because it's almost Easter," said Alice.

Finally, it was time to clean up and call it a night. Alice finished wiping down the counters and tables after the last ANGEL had left. She was about to turn out the lights, when she suddenly had a realization that filled her with guilt. *Goodness*, she thought, *there Mark is, possibly still recovering from surgery, maybe in pain, and I haven't even thought about him once.* Of course, she told herself that it was like that when she was doing things with the ANGELs. She so enjoyed these girls that she often forgot about the pressures of the day. To make up for her neglect, she said a quick prayer for Mark's recovery as she hurried back toward home.

She saw Mark's Range Rover parked in front of the inn, which under the circumstances she felt Louise would overlook. After all, the poor man had just been released from the hospital.

She went into the inn, pausing to remove her raincoat, then went off in search of Mark. She found Louise in the living room.

"Hello," said Louise as she looked up from her book. "How was ANGELs tonight?"

"Great," said Alice. "I noticed Mark's car."

Louise nodded and set her book aside. "They got here shortly after you left."

"How is he doing?"

"He has turned in for the night," said Louise. She wore a sober expression that hinted that there was more to her statement than its surface meaning.

Alice sat down in the chair across from her. "Was he feeling okay?"

"He said he was on some pain medication."

Alice nodded. "Probably worn out."

"Actually, he sat here for a bit. He wanted to wait up for you."

"That was sweet, but I'm glad he went to bed if he was tired."

"I think he was more angry than tired."

"Angry?" Alice leaned forward. "What do you mean?"

"I mean he and Adam got into it again."

"Oh dear." Alice glanced toward the open doorway, concerned that someone might overhear them.

"Don't worry, I'm fairly certain that everyone besides Jane, you and me has gone to bed."

"What happened?"

"Apparently, Mark was not impressed by Adam's driving skills, or rather lack thereof."

"Oh dear."

"I could tell that he was distraught when they came in. They were barely in the door when Mark mentioned something about Adam's driving and Adam got defensive."

"Hey, you two," said Jane as she entered the room. Then, lowering her voice, "Are you telling Alice about the fireworks?"

Louise frowned. "Yes."

Jane sat down next to Louise. "It was pretty nasty, Alice."

"Well, please, tell me what happened."

"Yes, I will," said Louise. "Adam got irate when Mark told him he needed to drive more safely."

"Adam told Mark to mind his own business," said Jane. "Well, not in those words exactly."

"Worse words," added Louise.

"Mark told Adam that since he was the passenger riding in his own vehicle that it was his business."

"Then Adam proceeded to tell Mark that he should be grateful that Adam was around to drive him from the hospital."

"And Mark told him that he wouldn't have needed to go to the hospital if Adam hadn't insisted on doing the climbing wall for so long."

"Oh dear."

"Yes, it just went from bad to ugly and then got worse." Louise shook her head. "In Mark's defense, he was in pain and under the influence of the medication."

"And he did feel bad when Adam left," added Jane.

"Adam left?"

"Oh yes. Adam went tearing upstairs, got all his belongings and stormed out of here like a cat with his tail on fire."

"Oh no . . ." Alice felt like crying. "Speaking of cats?"

"Adam took the kitten with him," said Jane.

"It doesn't seem that he will be coming back," said Louise.

To Alice's dismay, her older sister seemed relieved. Alice could not really blame Louise, but she did feel sorry for Adam.

"Where did he go?" she asked.

Louise just shrugged.

"Probably to wherever he was before," said Jane. "At least it's not winter. He won't freeze to death."

"But out there in the night?" said Alice. "Living in his car?"

"It's his choice, Alice." Jane stood. "Sorry, I need to go check on the eggs."

"I know it sounds hard," continued Louise. "But perhaps it is for the best."

How could it possibly be for the best? Alice thought. *How could Adam living out on the streets and Mark feeling guilty be for the best?* She kept these thoughts to herself and, thanking Louise for filling her in, she excused herself to go to bed.

Of course, she did not feel a bit like sleeping, once she was up there. Instead, she fell to her knees and begged God somehow to undo this horrible mess.

Protect Adam, she prayed. *Please, show him the way home.* Then she said, "Amen," and climbed into bed, trusting that things would be better tomorrow.

Chapter  Twenty

"How are you feeling this morning?" Alice asked Mark when she discovered him sitting by himself in the dining room. It was quite early and no other guests appeared to be up yet. She had been helping in the kitchen but suspected that Jane would excuse her for a few minutes. In fact, knowing Jane, she would probably be unhappy if Alice did not speak with Mark.

He looked up at her and attempted what appeared to be a halfhearted smile. "I've been better."

"Coffee?"

"Please."

She filled a cup and handed it to him. "I heard about the disagreement you and Adam had last night."

"It was more than a disagreement, Alice."

She nodded and sat down. "Yes, I know."

"And although I know that I didn't handle things properly, I think it may have been for the best."

Alice said nothing, just waited for him to continue.

"I feel that I've bent over backward for that kid. I know that he's unhappy, and I understand that he has good reason to be. But, honestly, I've done everything I can think of to get him to—oh, sometimes I don't even know what it is I'm trying to get him to do." Mark pushed his fingers through his beard and sighed loudly.

"To trust you?" she offered.

He looked at her over his coffee cup. "Yes, maybe that's it."

"Good morning," said Mrs. Winston as she and Laura entered the room.

Alice and Mark both turned and greeted them.

"How's your arm?" asked Mrs. Winston.

"Hurts a bit, but that's to be expected."

"Maybe you should take some more of those *wonderful* pain pills," said Laura in a clearly sarcastic tone.

"*Laura,*" said Mrs. Winston in a warning tone.

Alice studied the slender girl's stance and the look of disdain behind today's tangerine-colored sunglasses. It was clear that Laura was angry.

"*What, Mother?*" Laura snapped. "Do you expect me to just pretend that I don't know what's going on? Act as if I'm *blind*?"

"Laura is feeling concerned for Adam," said Mrs. Winston quickly.

"I'm blind, Mother, not deaf, and I don't need an interpreter."

"Maybe we should go for a walk," said Mrs. Winston, obviously uncomfortable with her daughter's behavior.

"No, that's okay," said Mark. "If Laura has something to say to me, she might as well get it off her chest. It's clear that she's angry with me."

"That's right," said Laura. "I am."

"Why is that?" asked Mark in a tired voice. "Is it because I told Adam the truth? Because I'm tired of playing games with him?"

"You don't even *know* him," said Laura. "You don't understand him at all. And, yes, I may be blind, but I see more than you do."

"*Laura!*"

"He asked me, Mother."

"But—"

"No, that's all right," said Mark patiently. "I'd like to know, Laura. What exactly is it that you think you can see in Adam? What is it that the rest of us are missing?"

"He's in pain," she told him. "He knew all along that you were going to cut him off like that. He knew that you never really cared."

"I did care," said Mark. "I do care, but how do you reach out to someone who keeps pushing you away?"

She folded her arms tightly across her chest and didn't answer.

"Really, Laura, I'd like to know. Somehow, you seem to have made an impression on Adam. You two seem to understand each other. What would you suggest I do differently?"

"What does it matter now?" She turned away. "I want to go back to our room, Mother."

Mrs. Winston seemed at a loss, but Alice looked her way with what she hoped was an encouraging smile. "It's okay," she told them both. "I think I understand why Laura is upset. You go on along. There's something I need to explain to Mark."

"Like he'll listen to you, or anyone for that matter," snapped Laura as she and her mother exited the room.

"Wow." Mark rubbed the cast on his arm with his good

hand. "I knew she was upset with me last night, but I had no idea she was this angry. I don't get it."

"That's what parents of teenagers say all the time," said Alice with a rueful smile.

"I wonder if it's possible to straighten this out with her."

"Oh, I'm sure it is, but there's something I'd like to tell you before you try." Alice paused at the sound of footsteps in the living room and realized that the Langleys were about to come into the dining room.

"How would you feel about going out for breakfast so that we can talk?" asked Alice.

"I'd love to."

"Okay," she said quickly. "I'll drive. Let me tell Jane."

"Meet you at the car?" asked Mark as he got up.

"Yes. But do you mind if I have a quick word with Laura first?"

"Not at all. I wish you would."

Alice explained her plans to Jane and Louise, who was helping Jane to prepare breakfast.

"No problem," said Jane. "It's about time you two got together and actually talked."

"Thanks."

"We were not trying to eavesdrop," began Louise in a tentative voice, "but it was impossible not to overhear Laura's outburst."

"It wasn't very nice," said Alice, "but Laura is partially right. Mark doesn't get the whole picture. I want to explain it to him."

"Don't be too hard on the poor guy," said Jane as she washed some blueberries. "He's been through a lot, you know."

"That's right." Louise paused from her stirring. "To be fair, this is mostly Adam's fault. He brought this onto himself."

"I don't think it's really about anyone's fault. It's really a series of misunderstandings," said Alice. "Before I leave I want to speak with Laura. She was very upset."

"That would be wise," said Louise. "We can't have our guests feeling miserable."

"There goes our little peacemaker," said Jane smiling fondly as she watched Alice leave the room.

∽

Alice tapped gently on the Garden Room door. "It's Alice," she said.

"Oh, Alice," said Mrs. Winston as she opened the door. "I'm so sorry about Laura's—"

"Don't apologize for me, Mother."

"If it's all right, I'd like to speak to Laura for a few minutes," Alice said.

Laura approached the door. "Is Mark with you?" she asked cautiously.

"No," Alice assured her, "it's just me. Do you want to come out in the hallway for a moment?"

Laura reached out and Alice took her by the hand, leading her to the open area at the top of the stairs. "I completely understand how you feel about the trouble between Mark and Adam, Laura."

"You do?"

"I do. I've wanted to explain some things to Mark myself, but I just never had the chance. I realize that Adam's behavior is really his way of protecting himself, of preventing himself from being hurt again."

Laura nodded eagerly. "Yes, that's true. You *do* get it."

"Mark and Adam have been gone so much. Then Mark broke his arm, and I was at my meeting last night. There just hasn't been an opportunity to talk to him." She sighed. "I feel that their disagreement is partly my fault."

"No," said Laura firmly. "It's Mark's fault. If you'd heard him last night, Alice, you'd agree. He never should've talked like that to Adam."

"You know, Mark is generally very even tempered, but he was upset," said Alice, "and I'm sure he was in pain. Then there was the effect of pain pills. Sometimes those pills cause people to let down their guard and say things they normally wouldn't say."

"Yeah, that's what my parents said too, but I still don't think it's an excuse. Adam is in a really fragile place right now."

"What do you mean?"

"He feels like he doesn't have much to live for. And even though he was pushing Mark away, I know that he was really hoping that Mark would somehow prove to him that he wanted to be involved in Adam's life. Kind of like a test. I think Adam was making Mark into his lifeline, but he wouldn't tell him, you know?"

Alice considered this. "You know, Laura, we can't expect another human being to be a lifeline. I mean it's good to have friends and family to lean on, but the only real lifeline is God."

Laura did not say anything.

"Even so," Alice went on quickly, "Adam must know that Mark is really there for him."

"But is he?"

"Of course."

"How do you know that for sure?"

"Well, I guess maybe I don't. But I'm going to spend some time with Mark this morning and I'll try to find out."

Laura sighed. "Well, I hope you knock some sense into that guy."

"Oh, Mark is sensible, Laura. It's just that he's never been a parent. You have to admit that Adam has been a little challenging for everyone."

"Hey, we're kids, ya know. That's what we do." Laura was smiling as she spoke.

"I hope you and your parents will feel comfortable about going down to breakfast now," said Alice. "I know that Jane and Louise are whipping up something special. If it helps to know, Mark and I are going out for breakfast."

"All right then." Laura nodded. "I'll get my parents." She smiled, and then added, "No use starving."

Alice found Mark waiting by her car. She quickly unlocked the doors and started to open the passenger side for him.

"I've still got one good arm," he told her.

"Sorry," she said. "I guess it comes with nursing. I'm just used to taking care of people."

"I didn't mean to growl at you," he said as he slid inside and then smiled sheepishly. "And to be honest, I'll probably need some help with the safety belt."

She reached across to grab the strap and fasten him in. Then, patting him on the head, she said, "Now, that's a good boy."

To her relief, he was actually smiling when she got inside. "You're good medicine, Alice."

"Thanks. I guess I chose the right profession."

Alice turned the radio on to her favorite jazz station. She would not bring up the subject of Adam until they reached the Coffee Shop and were settled. She suspected that Mark welcomed this brief reprieve too.

∞

"Hey there," called Hope Collins, the Coffee Shop's waitress, when they entered the restaurant. "How are you two doing?" Then she saw Mark's arm. "Oh dear, what happened to you, Dr. Graves? Get into an arm wrestling match with a sick polar bear?"

He smiled. "Yeah, something like that."

Alice quickly explained the climbing wall injury, and Hope nodded. "You know, I heard about that place and had actually been thinking about trying that out for myself, but now I might reconsider."

"I think I was just getting overconfident," admitted Mark as she led them to a table in the corner by the window. "I'd scaled it several times and done pretty well. Then Adam got the brilliant idea of timing ourselves to see who was faster."

"Oh dear," said Alice. "And you fell for that challenge?"

"Literally."

This made all three of them laugh. Hope handed them menus and told them about the breakfast special of steak and eggs.

"That sounds great to me," said Mark as he returned the menu.

Alice ordered a bowl of oatmeal with fresh fruit. Hope went back to the counter, but not without discreetly winking at Alice before she did.

Alice decided to get right to the point. She quickly told Mark about the touching scene she had witnessed between Adam and Laura. "It was so sweet, Mark," she said. "He was really sharing his feelings with her, and she told him how much his friendship was helping her. It's as if something amazing was beginning to happen."

"Until I cut it short."

"You can't take all the blame, Mark. Adam was testing you in every way he could."

"All because he didn't think I'd stick by him?"

She nodded. "He said that everyone left him eventually. He blamed himself for it."

"You know, he said something like that to me when we visited his parents' graves. He said that he'd been acting like such a jerk that his parents might still have been angry when they had their accident—or something to that effect. Of course, I told him that was ridiculous and, to be honest, I didn't even take him seriously, but now that I think about it, I wonder if he might actually be carrying a load of guilt about his parents' death. People do that, you know."

"Yes," she agreed. "Guilt is one of the stages of grieving."

"But how long does it last?"

"That depends on the person," she told him. "Some people get stuck in a stage and it takes a long time for them to move on."

"Well, Adam certainly seems stuck."

Hope brought their order, refilled Mark's coffee cup and refreshed Alice's hot water. "Just holler if you need anything else."

They continued talking as they ate. Their topic was mainly about Adam. When they were finished, Mark seemed encouraged. Yet, at the same time, he seemed troubled.

"Are you feeling okay?" asked Alice after he paid the bill.

He shrugged as he struggled to replace his billfold into his pocket. Alice waited.

"Bye, you two," called Hope as they went out the door.

"Is your arm hurting?" asked Alice when they reached the car.

"A little bit." He frowned. "More than that, I'm feeling bad about Adam now. I really came on strong last night. I'm sure the accident took a toll on his emotions as well. And, if the truth be told, the Range Rover probably presented a big temptation to see what it could do."

"Yes, I'm sure that I would barely keep from challenging other drivers to a race," Alice joked.

Mark managed a smile.

"Seriously, Mark, I think you did what most people would do—especially if you consider your day and that you were under the influence of pain pills."

"Maybe." He opened the door of the car, then climbed in and waited patiently for Alice to buckle him in again.

"There you go," she told him as she closed the door.

"Speaking of pain pills," he said as she started the engine. "I think I'm overdue now. I got up quite early and took one before six."

"Well, that's more than four hours," she noted. "We better get you home."

"Thanks, doctor."

"No problem, doctor." She turned and grinned. "Then I would recommend you have a little rest. There is nothing like rest to help you mend."

"Once again, I think you're right."

Chapter  Twenty-One

M ark came back downstairs just before noon.
"Feeling better?" asked Alice as she straightened the
rug in the foyer, then stood up.

"Somewhat. At least I'm rested. But I'm feeling worse
and worse about Adam. The idea of him and that kitten out
there living in his car . . . well, let's just say it's not a happy
thought. I have to go looking for him," said Mark.

"Not with one arm, you can't."

He looked pleadingly at her. "Could I interest you in—"

"You couldn't stop me if you wanted to."

"How about if we take my rig?" said Mark. "I filled it
with gas yesterday in Potterston."

"Let me get a jacket," she told him.

By the time Alice came back downstairs, Laura was in
conversation with Mark, and, to Alice's relief, it seemed much
more agreeable than the one earlier that day. Mark was asking
if Laura had any idea where they should look for Adam.

"I wish I could be more help," she told him.

"Don't worry. You've already been helpful."

"Do you want me to come too?" asked Laura. "In case I
think of something."

"You may if you'd like," said Mark. "If your parents don't mind."

She considered this. "Well, maybe I better not. My mom was in touch with a relative who still lives near Acorn Hill." She made a face. "We're supposed to be going to her house for tea this afternoon. Like that should be fun."

"You never know," said Alice.

Laura turned toward Alice with a hopeful expression. "Dr. Graves said you are going to look for Adam now."

"That's right."

"I wish I had some idea where he might be," said Laura. "But when I went places with him, well, I didn't really pay attention to where we went, you know."

"That's understandable," said Mark.

"Well, good luck," said Laura.

Alice and Mark headed out to his Range Rover. Dark clouds seemed to be gathering quickly, and Alice felt certain that they would be driving through a deluge before long.

"I told Laura that I realized what a complete fool I'd been, and I asked her to forgive me."

"Did she?"

He nodded. "Of course. You know, she's a sweet girl. She's just going through her own hard times and, Adam was actually helping her to work through some things."

"I know. Despite how things may appear, I think she made some real progress this week."

"She said the reason she got angry was because she felt so sorry for Adam, and she is seriously worried about the kitten too. Naturally, she focused her anger on me. Not that I blame her."

They started out looking for Adam's beat-up car around town. "At least it should be easy to spot," said Alice after they checked along the local main roads and parks. "But I'm guessing he's not in Acorn Hill."

"You're right. Why don't we check Potterston?"

It began raining as she got onto the highway. "This really is a nice vehicle," she told Mark. "It feels very safe in the rain."

"Range Rovers are hard to beat," he conceded. "I'll admit they're not cheap, but having been single all these years, well, I always gave myself permission to indulge in the best."

Alice thought about what he had said. She, too, had been single, but she had not embraced that particular philosophy.

"I suppose that sounds selfish to you," said Mark. "To be honest, it sounds a bit selfish to me now that I've verbalized it."

"Oh well . . ."

"You know, the more I think about everything, well, the more I realize that I have led a fairly self-centered and self-indulgent life." He exhaled loudly as he sadly shook his head. "And it's not a very comfortable realization."

"But think about all the animals you've helped."

He laughed. "Yes, all my animal friends, what would they do without me?"

"Your work is important."

He just turned and stared out the side window. "Important to me perhaps, but it was simply doing what I loved. Good grief, Alice, I did what I wanted, when I wanted, without ever considering anyone else."

"Oh, now that's probably an exaggeration."

"I don't think so. Consider that I was barely involved in my best friend's life for the past ten years. And my own god-son, Alice, look at the way I ignored that boy all this time."

"But his parents were still alive."

"Yes, but I should've remained a part of their lives."

Alice didn't know how to respond. On one hand, she agreed with Mark. Perhaps he had led a somewhat self-centered life. On the other hand, doing what you like to do in life is a gift and not necessarily selfish. She had devoted much time and energy to her father's ministry and to the church, but the truth was she had done it because it was what she had wanted to do with her life. It was not as if she had given anything up for it. In reality, she had only gained by giving. The people in her community had always respected her for her commitment to her father, and she had to admit that she liked that. In some ways, her lifestyle and choices could be considered just as selfish as Mark's.

But when she tried to explain this to him, he simply laughed.

"Oh, Alice," he said. "Dear, sweet Alice. I don't believe you have a selfish bone in your body."

"Ah, you don't know that, Mark." She turned the windshield wipers up several notches, to combat the sheets of rain that were pelting the car. There was a long pause while Alice focused her attention on navigating Mark's Range Rover down the nearly flooded highway.

"Do you ever wonder why neither of us married, Alice?" Mark asked.

Her hands gripped the wheel more tightly, partly because of the weather and partly because of his question. "Well, on occasion . . ." she finally said.

"Well, I've wondered about it a lot," he continued. "The truth is I never really figured it out. Sometimes I believed it was because God was saving us for each other—and for the right timing. Sometimes I believed it was simply because we both prefer not being married."

She nodded. "I've had similar thoughts."

"So which do you think it is, Alice?"

She slowed down as they caught up with a truck that was spewing a wake of water behind it. "I really don't know, Mark."

"I'm sorry," he said suddenly. "Here you are driving through this torrential rainstorm and I'm asking you all these tough questions. I'm sorry, Alice, we'll table this discussion for a better time. For now, we should focus our attention on the road and on finding Adam. Right?"

"You're absolutely right."

The rain let up when they reached Potterston, and after they had scoured the streets of Potterston, they started to feel that their search was useless.

"It's like finding a needle in a haystack," Mark said sadly after they finally turned back toward Acorn Hill.

"It's hard to find someone who doesn't want to be found."

"But maybe he wants to be found," suggested Mark.

"Then, I would think we'd find him."

"Yes, you're probably right."

"Maybe he's back at the inn," said Alice hopefully.

"I guess that's possible." Mark did not sound convinced.

When they got back to the inn, they found that Adam had not returned or called or been seen by anyone. Mark decided to go to his room to rest, and Alice went to help Jane in the kitchen. "You know what's funny," said Jane as Alice stood at the sink, peeling carrots.

"What?"

"Even Laura's parents looked for Adam today."

"Really?"

"Yes. Laura told me. They went all around Acorn Hill looking for him this afternoon, after they had tea."

"That's sweet." Alice picked up another carrot.

"Yes, I guess we are all worried about him."

Alice felt a lump form in her throat as she thought about poor Adam and Boots living in a smelly, damp car.

"He'll be okay, Alice."

"I hope so. Mark tried calling Adam's grandmother when we got home, but she said she hasn't seen Adam in ages."

"God knows where he is, Alice."

Alice brightened. "You know, you're right about that."

"Hey," Jane said, observing Alice's smile, "now there's a nice change."

Chapter  Twenty-Two

Good Friday dawned cloudy and gray, but according to Jane, the forecast called for clearing later in the day. "The weatherman said we'd have some blue skies by this afternoon," she told Alice as she put a pan of cinnamon rolls into the oven. "And it should be nice for the weekend."

"Oh good. That's a relief." Alice filled the teapot with hot water.

"Did you have a good walk?"

"Yes, but we cut it short. Vera is preparing for family coming for the weekend. That reminds me, has Louise heard whether Cynthia's coming or not?"

"Yes, she called yesterday and she can't make it, but she promised to come down in a couple of weeks."

Alice slapped her forehead. "Oh my! Jane, I'm so sorry. I forgot to tell you that I invited a guest for dinner tomorrow night."

"That's fine. Who did you invite?"

As Alice stemmed a basket of strawberries, she explained about the unexpected meeting with her old college friend Mattie. "I had not seen her since school," she told Jane. "And she wanted to come over to Acorn Hill for the egg hunt, and well, it just seemed right to invite her to dinner. I hope you don't mind. I'm sorry that I didn't tell you sooner, but so much has been happening it just slipped my mind."

"No problem," said Jane. "I was already planning something special anyway."

"And, of course, I'll help you."

"Tell me about Mattie," said Jane as she sliced a melon in half.

Alice wondered where to begin, and finally decided just to be honest and tell Jane her candid impressions of her old friend.

"Oh my," said Jane. "Four husbands?"

"Well, she did admit to having poor taste in men." Alice pulled the stem off a big strawberry, which she placed into the strainer. "Although she seemed to fully approve of Mark."

"Goodness," said Jane. "I hope you haven't invited trouble along with Mattie."

"Oh, I hardly think so."

"Don't be so naive, Alice. If this Mattie has gone through four husbands, she might think nothing of snatching a nice-looking, successful man from you."

"Oh, Jane." Alice rinsed the stemmed strawberries in cold water. "That's not fair to say. You don't even know her. Besides, do you really think Mark's the sort of man who would go for someone like that?"

"Maybe not, but that probably won't stop her from trying."

Alice really didn't feel concerned. If Mark could be so easily snatched, as Jane put it, then perhaps it would be for the best. Alice knew Mark well enough to believe that Jane's scenario was unlikely.

Breakfast that morning was as somber as the weather, for

everyone seemed a bit down. Alice knew her reasons for being quiet had to do with Adam, and she assumed the same was true for Mark and Laura.

Finally, Mr. Langley asked, "Has anyone heard anything from our missing young man?"

Both Mark and Alice looked at the older gentleman with surprise.

"We've been praying for him," explained Mrs. Langley. "We know that he's troubled and, well, we've felt bad for him."

"Thank you for praying for him," said Mark. "Although we've looked for him, we haven't any clues to his whereabouts."

"We looked for him yesterday as well," said Mrs. Winston. "Just around town."

"Yes," said Mark. "I heard about that, and I appreciate it."

"We thought we'd keep an eye out for his car when we head west today," said Mr. Langley. "You never know."

"Thank you," said Alice. "The more people looking for him, the more likely we are to find him."

After the guests had finished their breakfasts and were preparing to leave the table, Louise reminded everyone that they were welcome to color eggs for the egg hunt. "We'll start at around two this afternoon, and we expect to finish before dinnertime."

"That sounds like fun," said Mrs. Winston. "I haven't colored eggs in years." She turned and looked at her daughter. "Do you remember when we used to do that?"

Laura just shrugged, then excused herself.

It was not long before the other guests followed her lead and only Alice, Louise and Mark remained in the dining room.

"Not a very cheerful bunch," observed Louise.

"I feel like I'm to blame," said Mark. "I'm so sorry. If I

hadn't asked Adam to meet me here, and hadn't then made such a mess of things, well, obviously everyone would be much happier."

"Not necessarily," said Louise. "Laura has been moody since the Winstons arrived last weekend."

"That's true," said Alice.

"I don't know why I thought bringing Adam here would help things," said Mark. "I guess I hoped that he would be as charmed with Acorn Hill as I am and that somehow it would bring him back to his senses. It seems I was wrong."

Jane emerged from the kitchen with a fresh pot of coffee. "More caffeine, anyone?"

Louise and Mark both had another cup and Alice poured herself a cup of tea, but no one said anything.

"We've got to think of some way to cheer this place up," said Jane. "It's not feeling very festive for Easter weekend."

Alice gave her a warning look. "We were just discussing that, Jane."

"Yes," said Mark. "I've been apologizing for being responsible for the pall of gloom that seems to be hanging over your inn."

Jane frowned. "But, really, what can we do to brighten things up?"

"Well, the egg dyeing should be fun," said Alice.

"And there's the egg hunt," offered Louise.

"I wonder what Father would say if he were here," said Jane.

"It's interesting that you ask that," Alice said. "Father was usually quite somber on Good Friday. He was very quiet and contemplative, spending time in his office, thinking about the Passion and how Jesus suffered on the cross. He usually wrote his Easter sermon on Good Friday."

Jane nodded. "You know, that's just what Pastor Ken was saying to me this morning. I ran into him while jogging and he was walking along with his head hanging down like he'd lost his best friend."

"He was simply thinking," said Alice.

"So perhaps it's right for us to be a bit more serious on this day," said Louise.

"As true as that may be," said Mark with his eyes on Alice, "I would still like to go looking for Adam again this morning."

"Driving with one arm?" asked Jane.

"I'd be happy to drive for you again," offered Alice.

Mark gave her a grateful smile. "Thanks."

"Will you be back in time for egg coloring?" asked Louise.

"Of course," said Alice.

They decided to try driving north. "Perhaps he's headed for the countryside north of here," said Mark. "He told me that his family vacationed up there."

"Then that's the direction we'll take," said Alice as she headed north on the interstate.

"Perhaps we can just check out camping or rest stops for some miles ahead." Mark sighed and leaned back into the seat. "I suppose it really is useless, isn't it?"

"We might get lucky," Alice said, "or perhaps God will help us."

"I could use some divine help," he admitted. "Sometimes I think I depend on Dr. Mark Graves more than I depend on God." He held up his broken arm. "Then something happens that makes me feel helpless and useless, and suddenly I remember I'm not supposed to do everything on my own."

Alice smiled. "I guess we all need a wake-up call occasionally."

"How about you, Alice?" He turned to watch her as she drove. "Do you ever need a wake-up call? You seem so stable and grounded to me."

She laughed. "Well, don't forget that appearances can be deceiving. As far as stable and grounded? Lately, I've been feeling anything but."

"Is that because of me?"

She shrugged.

"And Adam?"

"Oh, I don't know. I think it's just life in general. And, really, isn't that what life is supposed to be, Mark? Surely, God never intended everything to move in a straight, unwavering line. What would be the point of that?"

"How did you get to be so wise, Alice?"

She smiled. "Well, if that were true, and I'm not sure that it is, I would have to give a lot of the credit to my father. He was the wisest person I have ever known."

He sighed. "I wish I'd gotten to know him better."

"You would've liked him, Mark."

"Yes, I'm sure. I suppose I've actually gotten to know him a bit through you. I'm quite sure that you're very much your father's daughter."

She laughed. "How could I not be?"

They drove for over an hour before they decided to turn back.

"I feel bad for wasting your time like this," said Mark.

"It's not a waste," said Alice. "I love road trips and your car is wonderful to drive." She smiled. "The company's not bad either."

"Really?" He sounded hopeful now. "I thought perhaps you would be sick of me by now. I feel as if I've brought you nothing but trouble for the past week." Mark pointed to an exit ahead. "Hey, why don't you turn there, Alice. As I recall there's a pretty good restaurant in this town. Maybe we could get some lunch."

She followed his directions, driving into a small town not unlike Acorn Hill. Soon they were parked in front of what appeared to be an historic inn. "This looks lovely," she told him as she handed him the keys.

"We could take a little stroll," he suggested. "Just to stretch our legs some."

They walked up and down the streets of the quaint little town. Mark told her a bit about his childhood and about the times that his family had stopped in this town while on their way to a lake to the north. "I remember my sister and I used to fight all the way and once my father actually threatened to leave us right here in this town."

Alice laughed. "Well, it's not such a bad spot to be abandoned. I'm sure some nice family would've adopted the two of you."

"I think I sometimes forget how important family is," he said. "I mean, I've led such an independent life. As hard as it was spending time with Adam, I really started to get a feeling of what it's like to have family. Even though it was hard, I think I rather liked it too. I mean, it had its moments."

"I'm sure you would've made a good dad, Mark."

"Do you think it's too late? I mean with Adam." He chuckled. "I don't exactly want to have children of my own."

Alice felt herself blushing. "No, I didn't think that's what you meant. But, really, I don't think it's too late with Adam."

"That is, if I ever see him again."

"I'm sure you will, Mark."

By now, they had gone all through town and were back

at the inn. The old building was as interesting on the inside as the exterior. With antiques that looked like they had been there for at least a couple hundred years, and waitresses who wore period costumes, Alice felt that she had actually gone back in time. The food was excellent, and by the time they were finished Alice was not sure she wanted to leave.

"This is a charming place," she told Mark. "I'm so glad you brought me."

"I thought you'd like it." He smiled as he held the door for her with his good hand. "It's not Acorn Hill, but it's got its pluses."

"Oh, I think that this town could give Acorn Hill a run for its money." She glanced down the cobblestone street. "But Acorn Hill has always been and always will be my home."

"I'd hoped to make it my home too," said Mark after they got into the car.

"Yes, I heard that you'd looked at the Olsen house," she said as she started the engine.

"You did, did you?" He chuckled. "Well, I guess it's hard to keep secrets in a town Acorn Hill's size."

"Especially when you have an Aunt Ethel."

He nodded. "An aunt who dates the mayor."

"Yes, you see what I mean."

"Things got so busy with Adam that I never had a chance to get back to the real estate agent."

She made no comment. This was none of her business.

"I rather liked the old house. Oh, I can see it needs lots of work, but I could imagine myself puttering around there, fixing things up. And then there's the carriage house in back that would be perfect for a small animal infirmary."

Part of her wanted to ask him how she fit into this picture, but another part of her was unsure that she wanted to hear that answer just now. So she just drove in silence.

After a bit, Mark turned on his radio. "What is that jazz station you listen to?" he asked as he played with the dial.

"It's 97.4 FM," she told him. "You should be able to get it from here."

He tuned it in to the smooth sounds of Miles Davis. "That's nice," he said. "I'm glad we like the same kind of music."

Alice did not tell him that she liked a variety of music and occasionally even listened to country, which Jane could not, for the life of her, understand. Louise didn't even know, thank goodness. But Alice didn't have to reveal everything about herself to Mark or anyone, besides God, for that matter. Perhaps it was good to have some secrets.

They got back to the inn just before two. "As much as we'd love your help with the eggs," said Alice as they walked up to the porch, "I'd recommend you have a rest first."

"I won't even argue with you," he said as he opened the door and waited for her to go inside.

Before he went upstairs, Mark asked whether anyone had seen or heard from Adam. Unfortunately, they had not. Alice tried not to notice the distinct slowness to Mark's steps as he went upstairs. She told herself it was simply because he was worn out, but she suspected it had more to do with disappointment.

At least the ANGELs brought some joy and levity to the egg dyeing party, and it was not long before Alice found herself laughing over things like rainbow-colored fingernails (when Ashley dyed her fingertips various colors) and other childish goings-on. Laura and her mother joined in, and

Alice appreciated how the ANGELs gravitated toward the teenaged girl, showing obvious admiration of her age, not to mention her cool, acid-green sunglasses. To everyone's delight, Laura seemed to warm up to the girls too, and didn't even mind them helping her.

Alice had privately informed them that Laura had become blind recently. Of course, this was of huge interest to them, and, being young, they had no qualms about asking her questions like, "Can you still remember what purple looks like?" and "Do you close your eyes when you get scared?" To everyone's relief and amusement, Laura actually answered them.

"This has been wonderful," said Mrs. Winston as she helped Alice tidy up. "Thank you for including us."

"Thank you for helping," said Alice. "Many hands make light work."

"Your ANGELs are delightful."

"They can get a bit silly sometimes, but I do enjoy them."

By four-thirty, the brightly colored eggs were all carefully placed back into their cartons and stored in the big refrigerator. All the egg dyers were treated to Jane's special Easter egg truffles as a thank you.

Although Mark had not come down yet, Alice saved one for him. She figured he might need something to lift his spirits, and Jane's chocolates were capable of doing just that.

Chapter  Twenty-Three

Just as Alice said good-bye to the last ANGEL, Mark appeared in the kitchen looking tired and downhearted. First, Alice offered him a chocolate egg, and then she invited him to take a walk with her. She could tell that Jane, who had been very patient with the egg dyeing, now wanted her kitchen back to herself, and Alice hoped that some fresh air might cheer up Mark.

"It's turned into a lovely day," she said as their long walk took them to the park where the festivities would take place the next day.

"Should be nice for the big egg hunt tomorrow." He glanced over at the empty bench in the park. "Want to sit for a bit?"

"Sure." She controlled herself from glancing over her shoulder as she and Mark walked across the grass toward the bench. She knew that if she and Mark were spied sitting together in this private but public place, the local tongues would be wagging before dinnertime. Still, she told herself, what did it matter?

Mark sat down and leaned forward in a dejected posture. She reached over and patted his back. "I know you're feeling bad," she said in an understanding voice. "I am too, but I've decided that it won't help anything to go around depressed. Instead, I'm praying for Adam. Every single time I think about him and begin to worry, I just put him in God's hands. As Jane reminded me this morning, we may not know where Adam is right now, but God does."

Mark sat up straighter and looked at her. "I know you're right, but my heart is still heavy."

"Have you been praying for him?"

He nodded.

"Then maybe we just need to believe that God is handling it."

He nodded again. "I'll try."

"Hi, Miss Howard," called a girl's voice from the street.

Alice looked up to see the girl waving wildly from her bicycle. "Hi, Ashley," Alice called back. Now she could be sure that word would get around about her and Mark. If anyone could jump to conclusions, it was Ashley.

"One of your ANGELs?"

Alice smiled. "Yes. They were so helpful today."

"Sorry I didn't make it down."

"It may have been a bit chaotic for you," she told him. "I'm glad you had a good rest."

"You know, Alice," he began, then stopped.

She waited without speaking.

"We need to talk . . . about us . . . you know."

Again, she said nothing.

"I want to, well, make my intentions clear, you know?"

"Intentions?"

"That's probably not the right word, but I feel as if I've been dancing all around this thing. That's partly because of what's been happening with Adam. I guess to be fully honest, I've had a case of chilly toes too."

She laughed. "Chilly toes?"

"Yes, they're not as severe as cold feet. I've been a bachelor my whole life, and I know that I'm self-centered and set in my ways. That's certainly been driven home well enough with my relationship with Adam. Anyway, I want to be perfectly honest with you."

"Yes?"

"Well, I just don't know what's going on in me right now." She smiled. "Join the club."

"Really?" He peered into her eyes. "You feel like that too?"

She nodded.

"Well, that's a relief." Then he took her hand with his good one. "I do have strong feelings for you, Alice. I'm just not sure of the timing."

"I understand."

"If this thing with Adam hadn't blindsided me, well, maybe it would be different. I don't know."

She patted his hand with her other one. "Perhaps we don't need to be too concerned about these things right now, Mark. I mean, really, we've waited this long. What's the hurry, right?"

He smiled. "Right."

"Now," she slipped her hand away from his, "before we become the talk of the entire town, although I suspect it's already too late, perhaps we should go home."

∞

They reached the inn and were walking up the steps to the front porch when Alice heard a man's excited voice. "Alice and Mark! Over here!"

They looked up to see Mr. and Mrs. Langley sitting together in the porch swing, and Mr. Langley was waving. "Come here," he called. "I have good news."

Alice and Mark went over to join the older couple.

"What is it?" asked Mark as he sat in the wicker rocker.

"It's about Adam," said Mrs. Langley.

"Yes," agreed Mr. Langley, "We're on our way back to the inn when I pull into a Shell station, and what do you know?"

"There, parked on the side street, was an old car that looked like Adam's," Mrs. Langley said.

"That's right," said Mr. Langley, "so I say to the missus, I say, you wait here while I check into this matter. I go over and sure enough, leaning back in the driver's seat of that run-down little car is a familiar-looking young man. So I knock on the window, giving the poor lad a start. But then he recognizes me and gets out of the car." He sadly shook his head. "And the boy looks worse than ever. But I tell him that everyone at the inn is looking for him."

"That's when I came over," said Mrs. Langley. "And poor Adam didn't believe my husband, so I jumped right in and straightened him out. I told him that we'd all been frantic with worry and that we'd all been looking."

"Well, he is pretty surprised," said Mr. Langley. "And he asks if Mark is looking and I tell him that Alice has been chauffeuring him all over the state and that even today you two are looking up north."

"And did he believe you?" asked Mark hopefully.

"He was still skeptical," said Mrs. Langley. "But we told him that he should come back to the inn and see for himself."

"And will he?" asked Alice.

Mr. Langley held up his hands in that way people do when they are unsure. "I don't really know whether he will or not."

"But we gave him some money," said Mrs. Langley. "His tank was empty and he was broke."

"And then we begged him to come back to the inn," said Mr. Langley.

"Thank you," said Mark. "I really appreciate it."

"I just hope he does," said Mrs. Langley. "He still has the kitten with him. He said not to worry, that he was taking good care of it."

"Probably better care of it than himself," offered Alice.

"No doubt," said Mrs. Langley.

"I guess all we can do is to pray now," said Mr. Langley.

"Do you think we should drive over?" asked Mark suddenly. "To talk to him?"

"I don't know what more you could say," said Mr. Langley.

"Maybe we should wait," said Alice, "let him come back on his own."

Mark nodded. "Maybe you're right. There's certainly no use forcing him."

"I suspect he's not the kind who likes to be forced," said Mr. Langley.

"Who does?" said Mark.

∽

Dinner was a bit more cheerful that evening. Mark and Alice filled in Jane and Louise on the details as the four of them dined in the comfort of the kitchen. Alice noticed that Mark kept glancing at the clock and out the window, as if he were waiting for someone, and of course, she knew that he was.

After dinner, Louise played piano while Jane and Alice put together a dessert of chocolate-covered cream puffs.

"How are things going with Mark?" asked Jane as she took the pastry shells from the oven.

Alice stirred the custard filling. "Does this look okay?" she asked, ignoring her sister's question.

Jane set the shells on a cooling rack. "That looks perfect," she said. Putting her hands on her hips in that I-mean-business stance, she then turned to Alice and said, "Come on, I've tried to be patient, but you're holding out on me. How's it going with Mark?"

Alice shrugged. "It's fine."

"That's not what I mean and you know it. Tell me what's going on with you guys. Come on, you promised you would."

Alice sighed. "Okay, it's not going anywhere. Does that answer your question?"

"But why?" demanded Jane.

"Oh, it has to do with the whole Adam thing," said Alice, "but there's more to it than that. I think it has to do with us—I just don't think we're ready to make any decisions."

Jane nodded and turned her attention to the chocolate sauce in the double boiler. "Okay," she said as she dipped in a spoon. "That makes sense. I know there's been a lot going on, and I can see that you might not want to make a commitment yet. What about later, when things settle down and Adam gets his life on track? What about then?"

"I honestly don't know."

Jane brought the spoon of chocolate sauce over to Alice. "How's this?"

Alice tasted the sauce, then smiled. "Decadent."

"Okay, then," said Jane, "you will let me know if things change between you and Mark."

Alice nodded. "You'll be the first to know—well, you and Louise both."

"Good." She returned to the stove and turned down the gas.

"Tell me, Jane," said Alice, "why do I feel as if you're pushing me toward Mark? Are you eager to get rid of me?"

Jane turned around wearing a shocked expression. "No,

Alice, that's not it at all. You know that I don't want to get rid of you. Selfishly, I'd like everything to stay just as it is, but I want you to be happy too."

"I am happy."

"You really care about Mark, Alice. I can see it."

"Yes, you're right, I do. I care about a lot of people."

"Not like that, Alice. You know what I mean."

"It's just not that simple, and, honestly, sometimes I'm not even sure how I feel."

"Well, as you said, it could be just the timing. There's no harm in waiting."

Alice laughed. "You make it sound as if Mark and I have some big kind of romantic plan to pull off. Really, Jane, trust me, we don't."

"I believe you." Jane set the chocolate pot into cold water to cool. "I just don't want to be out of the loop if you ever do."

Soon they had the cream puffs constructed, and Alice was topping them with dollops of whipped cream. "These are going to disappear before our very eyes," she told Jane. "No one can resist your cream puffs."

She was right. Not only did they disappear but Mark had more than one. For some reason that gave Alice hope that his spirits were improving. Still, she prayed long and hard for Adam before she went to bed that night. She prayed for his safety and she prayed for his heart.

Please, let him be like the prodigal son, she prayed. *Let him see that it is time to come home and then help him to humble his heart so he can do it.*

Chapter Twenty-Four

Saturday morning was a flurry of activity at the inn. Alice helped Jane with breakfast and its cleanup, as well as the preparations for the picnic that would follow the egg hunt. She had already made her apologies to Mark, explaining that she would probably be busy until after the egg hunt. They had agreed to meet then.

The ANGELs arrived at the inn and were standing in the foyer, when Jenny spotted Laura and her mother in the parlor. "Can Laura help us hide eggs, Miss Howard?" asked Jenny.

Alice glanced at Mrs. Winston, not sure that this plan would work. "Of course," she said. "Laura is welcome to help us if she wants to."

"Oh, I don't think—" Mrs. Winston began.

"Why not, Mother?" said Laura.

"Well, if you'd like to . . ."

Jenny pulled another set of bunny ears from her bag and ran over to take Laura's hand. "You have to wear bunny ears like the rest of us," she said as she reached up and arranged them on Laura's head, careful not to disturb the hot pink sunglasses that Laura was sporting.

"They look cool with your glasses," said Jenny, "the fuzzy white outsides are lined with pink satin on the insides."

Laura reached up and felt the furry ears that were attached to the headband and grinned. "Just call me Peter—no, Mopsy—Cottontail."

"All right, Mopsy," said Ashley. "We better hit the bunny trail."

Sissy gave Laura one of the prize baskets to carry, happily explaining to her what it was and how the ANGELs had put them all together themselves.

"There are ten prize baskets," said Jenny as they all trooped out of the inn wearing bunny ears.

"We'll meet you at the park with the eggs and stuff," called Jane as Alice followed along behind the girls.

The ANGELs started singing as they walked, changing the words of "The Ants Go Marching" to "The Bunnies Go Marching," and to Alice's pleased surprise, Laura sang right along with them.

By the time they reached the park, Jane and Louise were already there. Jane was setting up a table and Louise was having what seemed to be an intense conversation with Ethel and Lloyd. Alice could tell by their faces that it was some kind of disagreement. Alice decided to pay them no mind. Surely, they would figure out whatever it was in time.

Louise came over to help her sisters. "Good grief," she said under her breath.

"What's up, Louie?" asked Jane as she spread a pretty, pastel print table cloth over the folding table.

"Well, Aunt Ethel has decided that Mr. Easter Rabbit should give the opening words at the beginning of the egg hunt."

"That's always been done by the pastor of Grace Chapel,"

said Alice. "I already asked Rev. Thompson to do the honors."

"Oh, Ken will understand," said Jane. "I can talk to him."

Louise frowned and shook her head. "Politics."

"Well, the children will probably like it," Alice assured her. "After all, it does seem fitting that a rabbit open the egg hunt. I don't know why we never thought of it before."

"Probably because Mr. Easter Rabbit only got his bunny suit a couple years ago," Louise said with an exasperated shake of her head. "Alice, is that Laura with your ANGELs?"

Alice laughed. "That's Laura. The girls wanted her to help them hide eggs."

Now Louise smiled. "Well, now that is something."

All the pretty prize baskets were lined up on the table, and every last egg hidden just before ten o'clock, when the festivities were due to begin. Mr. Easter Rabbit gave his opening words, and everyone cheered—even Louise.

"Don't worry," Pastor Ken had assured Jane after she had told him the news. "I'll get my chance to be up front tomorrow."

The children were divided into five different age groups, with the toddlers starting first and with the ten-year-olds ending the hunt. The prize eggs were hidden in areas restricted to the various age groups, with the ANGEL bunnies and Mr. Easter Rabbit paying close attention lest any of the older children try to sneak into one of the younger sections. Alice noticed that Jenny was still holding onto Laura's hand, and it looked as if both of them were having a good time.

While Alice was manning the prize station, she noticed a woman walking across the park toward them. Alice did not recognize her at first, although she felt certain, because of the shiny gold suit, that this woman was not a local. It also caught Alice's attention that this woman was not accompanied by a child. As she got closer, Alice realized it was Mattie Singleton.

She waved at Mattie, but her old friend must not have seen her for she suddenly turned and walked toward the spectator area, straight to where Mark and her sisters were seated in the lawn chairs that they had brought from home. Well, that was fine. Alice had her hands full for the next hour anyway. They would take care of Mattie.

Eggs were found, a few tears were shed and the much coveted prize baskets awarded. Then it was finally time to move on to the picnic portion of the day's event. Alice was happy to be relieved of her responsibilities as she went over to join her sisters, Mark and Mattie.

"Alice!" Mattie waved to greet her. "I simply adore your little town. The Easter egg hunt was like something out of a Norman Rockwell painting. That funny old Easter Bunny and the little girl bunnies helping the children. Oh, it was just too sweet."

"I'm so glad you came," said Alice as she sat in the empty chair next to Jane. "I see you've met my sisters."

Mattie smiled. "Yes, they've been making me feel right at home."

"I hope you'll join us for lunch, Mattie," said Louise. "We have more than enough."

"I'd love to." Mattie smiled at Mark. "You were absolutely right, Mark. Acorn Hill is a charming, delightful place. I almost feel as if I've been transported back in time. It reminds me of the fifties, back when we were young and life was simple."

Louise handed each person a plate and Alice poured cups of lemonade while Jane began to arrange the food on a small folding table.

"Let me help you with that, Mark," offered Mattie when Alice attempted to hand him his drink. Mattie scooted her chair closer to Mark and took the drink for him.

"Everything gets a lot trickier when you have only one good arm," he said as Mattie helped him to put his cup in the drink holder.

"I'll get your food for you too," said Mattie as she took his paper plate.

Jane eyed Alice curiously, but Alice simply acted as if she were preoccupied with opening a jar of pickles.

"Hello there," called Ethel as she led Lloyd, or rather Mr. Easter Rabbit, over to where they were sitting. "May we join you?"

"Oh my!" cried Mattie happily. "Do we really get to have lunch with the Easter Bunny?"

"Mr. Easter Rabbit," corrected Ethel.

"Otherwise known as Lloyd Tynan," said Louise in a hushed tone. "The mayor of Acorn Hill." Then she introduced Mattie to them.

"Welcome to our town." Lloyd bowed graciously.

"This is too precious," gushed Mattie. "Mr. Easter Rabbit himself. Oh, I wish I'd brought my camera."

They began loading their plates with fried chicken, potato salad and the other goodies that Jane had packed. Mattie remained on hand to assist Mark, and Alice tried to act as if she didn't mind. Then once her plate was filled, she simply sat back in the chair, focused her attention on the picnic crowd all around them and ate her lunch.

"This potato salad is delicious," said Mattie.

"That's Jane's special recipe," said Louise.

"It's a version of German potato salad," said Jane.

"It's yummy." Mattie turned to Mark. "Can I get you another serving? You seem to have enjoyed it too."

Mark looked uncomfortable. Alice suspected Mattie's attention embarrassed him, but then he admitted he would like more, and Mattie hopped up and got it for him.

Jane turned her head away from them so that only Alice could see and mouthed, "What is going on?"

Alice just shrugged, then said, "There are the Humberts." She waved and called hello, then turning back to Jane, asked, "Where are the Langleys and the Winstons? I thought perhaps they would join us."

Jane pointed across the park. "They're over there. Mrs. Winston's cousin invited them to share a picnic and the Winstons invited the Langleys."

Alice smiled. "How nice."

Jane still looked agitated, but Alice pretended not to notice, and as soon as her plate was empty she excused herself. "I'm going to go talk to the Humberts," she said. She felt relieved to get away from her little picnic group. It was unsettling to see Mattie cozying up to Mark, but Mark was a grown man. He could surely deal with the situation.

"Alice," said Vera. "Come join us."

"I just thought I'd say hello." Alice said. She chatted for a bit, then went around greeting and visiting with others in the crowd.

"Those prize baskets were wonderful," said Sylvia. "Little Leo Andrews showed me his and it was very impressive. Good job."

Alice smiled. "I guess it pays off to send out a letter in advance."

Sylvia lowered her voice now. "Where is Dr. Graves?"

"He's over there eating with my sisters and some friends."

"Everything okay?"

Alice nodded. "Of course." She continued making her rounds. By the time she got back, only her sisters were there, packing things up.

"Where have you been?" asked Louise.

"Just visiting," said Alice.

"Well, Aunt Ethel and Lloyd went home. Lloyd had a headache. Then Mattie begged Mark to give her a tour of the town, and he finally gave in and agreed."

"That's nice." Alice forced a smile to her lips.

"That's nice?" Jane stood up and looked at Alice with raised eyebrows. "You think that's nice? Mattie may be determined to make Mark husband number five and you think that's nice?"

Louise blinked. "Husband number five?"

"That's right," said Jane. "Didn't Alice tell you that Mattie goes through men like Kleenex?"

"Well, no . . ." Louise looked at Alice. "Goodness, I don't believe that I have even owned five cars in my lifetime. Five husbands?"

"Only four," said Alice.

"That's right," said Jane as she closed the picnic basket. "Mark would be number five."

"Oh, Jane." Alice went over and put her arm around Jane's shoulders. "Don't worry so much. Mark is a grown man. He's able to take care of himself."

"It's not Mark I'm worried about," said Jane. "It's you."

Alice smiled. "I'm fine, Jane. Really." Then she began folding up the chairs and table and helped her sisters to load things back into Louise's car. "You go ahead without me," said Alice. "I'd like to walk home."

"By way of town?" asked Jane hopefully.

Alice shook her head. "I just want to enjoy this lovely day."

Jane gave Alice a look that seemed to question Alice's sanity. Alice decided to pay her no mind. She hummed to herself as she walked back toward the inn. *Really*, she asked herself, *why should I be concerned?*

Chapter  Twenty-Five

W hen Alice reached the inn, she was surprised and delighted to see a familiar car parked not in front, but in back. She knew that beat-up old Nissan had to belong to Adam, and she could barely keep from running as she hurried inside.

"You came back!" she practically cried when she saw him standing in the foyer with Jane and Louise.

Louise smiled at Alice. "Adam was just apologizing for the trouble he caused."

Alice went straight to Adam and threw her arms around him. "I'm so glad you came back, Adam." She hugged him tightly, not caring whether he minded or not, and finally she let him go and stepped back. She could tell he was embarrassed by her display of affection, but at the same time he seemed to appreciate it.

"I'm sorry I was such a jerk to you, Alice," he told her.

"Never mind about that," said Alice. "I'm so glad that you came back. Do you know how much we all missed you?"

He looked down at the floor. "That's what the Langleys said, but I wasn't really sure."

"Well, be sure," said Alice. "Mark and I looked all over

for you. So did the Winstons. Laura's been just sick with worry for you."

"And the kitten," said Jane. "How's Boots?"

"I better go get him," said Adam quickly. "I left him in the car. Just in case . . . you know. I put the window down so he wouldn't get too hot."

"Yes," said Alice. "Do go get him."

"There are leftovers from the picnic," added Jane, "fried chicken and potato salad. Come in the kitchen when you're ready."

For the first time, Alice thought she almost caught Adam smiling.

"Thanks," he said as he started to head out, then paused. "Where's Mark?"

"Oh, he's showing an old friend the town," said Alice. "He should be back soon."

Adam nodded and went out.

"Isn't it wonderful," said Alice to her sisters.

"I hope so," said Louise with a slightly skeptical expression. "Let's just hope that he's sincere."

"Oh, I'm sure he is," said Alice.

"I think so too," agreed Jane. "Maybe that little stint out on his own helped him to see things differently."

"Let's hope so."

Alice walked Adam up to his room and waited as he got Boots settled in. "That cat is lucky to have you, Adam," she said as they left the room.

"I don't know . . ." He turned and looked at her. "I mean Mark was kind of right. I can barely take care of myself."

"Maybe you just need some help." She reached over and patted his shoulder. "It's not much fun to be all on your own, is it?"

He shook his head. "You got that right."

"Well, I know we got off to a rocky start, Adam, but I'd really like to be your friend."

"Yeah, I know. I think I was just jealous of you."

"Of me?"

"You know, it's like you were getting Mark's attention, and I was acting like a spoiled brat. Pretty dumb, huh?"

She smiled. "We all make mistakes, Adam. The best thing is to realize what we're doing wrong and try to make it right."

"Yeah, that's what I'm hoping."

Alice felt more hopeful than ever as they went into the kitchen. It really seemed that things had changed, or were changing, with Adam. Why else would he come back here and apologize? Besides, she reminded herself as she filled a plate with picnic leftovers for him, one should always think the best of a person. Of course, she wondered if she could also apply this philosophy to Mattie Singleton.

Adam was just finishing his meal when the Winstons came back to the inn. Alice met Laura at the door with the good news.

"Where is he?" asked Laura.

"Right here," said Adam as he emerged from the dining room. Then he walked right up to the Winstons and apologized for being so disrespectful.

Mr. Winston looked surprised, but he reached out and shook Adam's hand. "Takes a man to say I'm sorry," he said.

Adam nodded, then looked away. Alice felt sorry for him. She knew this couldn't be easy.

"Where's Boots?" asked Laura eagerly.

"I'll go get him," said Adam. "Want to meet me on the porch?"

The afternoon settled into a relaxed pace with Adam and Laura playing with Boots on the front porch, and Mr. Langley and Mr. Winston enjoying a game of chess in the library, while their wives visited with Louise in the parlor. Alice went to the kitchen to help Jane get some things ready for dinner.

"Wouldn't you think that Mark and Mattie would be back by now?" asked Jane as she rubbed a leg of lamb with lemon juice, salt and pepper, and began studding it with garlic.

"Depends on how much of the town Mattie wanted to see," said Alice.

"And it doesn't bother you in the least?"

"Oh, Jane." Alice sighed. "Of course, it bothers me."

"Well, that's a relief." Jane smiled. "I thought maybe aliens had snatched you and performed a lobotomy or something. I'm not involved with Mark the way that you are, but it bothers me a lot."

"There's not much I can do about it, Jane. I can't see how it makes anything better to feel unhappy."

"Maybe not, but I think that Mattie has some kind of nerve."

"In all fairness, I told her last week that Mark and I were only just friends."

"Even so."

"And, really, that's all we are, Jane."

"Yeah, but . . ."

"We shouldn't judge Mattie."

"Maybe not, but—"

"Speaking of whom," Alice said, holding a finger to her lips, "I think I hear them now."

"Go and see."

Alice slipped out in time to see Mark and Adam talking in the foyer, and then embracing. She sighed in relief. Well, at least that was over. Then Mark was introducing Adam to Mattie and, despite her earlier words to Jane, Alice felt a small twinge of jealousy. Perhaps she was imagining things, but it seemed as if Mattie had suddenly stepped into the role of Mark's girlfriend.

Alice retreated into the kitchen.

"What's going on?" asked Jane.

Without mentioning her feelings about Mattie, Alice described the reunion of Mark and Adam.

"Oh, that's good," said Jane as she slid the lamb into the oven. "I think we're done in here, at least for the time being, if you'd like to go visit with Mark now."

Alice said nothing.

Jane frowned as she hung up her apron. "Come on, Alice. What's up?"

She just shook her head. "I don't know . . ."

Then Jane took Alice by the shoulders, turned her around so she was facing the door and gave her a gentle shove. "Get out of here, Alice. Go and talk to him."

Feeling like a six-year-old, Alice obeyed. She could hear the voices of Louise and the other women coming from the parlor, and the two men were still playing chess in the library. Looking out the window, she saw that Mark and Mattie had joined Laura and Adam on the porch. Mattie was holding the kitten and the four of them looked so natural and comfortable out there that Alice could not bring herself to interrupt them.

Instead, she went upstairs. She knew without a doubt that she had taken the coward's way out. She also knew that she was just plain tired, and so she took a nap.

When she woke, it was time to help Jane with dinner. First, she freshened up and, determined to put on a brave face, she even changed into a festive outfit—a rich-toned paisley skirt and a sage green silk blouse. She even put on a couple pieces of Jane's handmade jewelry.

"There," she said to her image in the mirror. "At least no one will suspect that you're feeling like a wallflower tonight."

"Look at you," said Jane when Alice came into the kitchen. "Very nice outfit."

Alice shrugged and smiled. "You mean this old thing?"

Jane laughed and handed her an apron. "I was with you when you got that old thing, Alice, and it was only a couple months ago."

They worked happily together in the kitchen for a while, and then Jane asked Alice to set the dining room table. Jane had insisted they use the best china and crystal tonight, along with candles and flowers. Alice was just lighting the candles when she heard footsteps.

"Lovely," said a deep voice from behind her.

She jumped and then turned to see Mark. "Oh, you startled me," she said, then blew out the match.

"My apologies."

She smiled. "It does look nice, doesn't it?"

"I wasn't talking about the room, Alice. Although I must admit that it looks lovely too."

She felt herself blushing and was glad that she had already adjusted the dimmer switch on the chandelier so that the lights were low. "Where's Mattie?" she asked as she straightened a napkin.

"Last I saw she was putting her feet up in the parlor," said Mark. "I think she was a bit worn out."

Suddenly Alice felt guilty for neglecting her own guest. "Perhaps I should go see if she needs anything."

"I just came in to see what time dinner will be," he said.

Alice glanced at her watch. "Jane said it should be ready around seven. Would you let Adam know?"

"Certainly." He smiled. "Isn't it great that he came back?"

"Yes, I was so glad to see him."

Just then Louise came into the dining room. "This looks very nice," she said after greeting them. Then Mark excused himself.

"I thought I would give Jane a hand," said Louise.

"But I'm already—"

"I think you should see to your guests," said Louise in a firm voice.

Alice sensed that she was referring to Mattie. "Thank you," she told her. "I'll do that."

Of course, Alice was not eager to be with Mattie, but she reminded herself that she was the one who had invited her to dinner.

"Hey, Alice," said Adam as he came down the stairs.

"Hi." She smiled at him, pleased that it appeared he had put a bit of effort into his appearance. Certainly, his shirt could have used a pressing and his trousers still looked to be ready to fall off, but at least his hair was neatly combed. "How's it going, Adam?"

He shrugged. "Okay, I guess."

"How is Boots?"

Adam sighed. "I've been thinking about him."

"What do you mean?"

"I've been thinking that I should give him to Laura."

"Is that what you want to do?"

"It might be the best thing to do."

She nodded, surprised that he was confiding in her like this. "I'm sure Laura would take good care of him."

"That's what I thought too. It's kind of hard having a cat when you live in a car."

"Are you going to keep doing that?"

He shrugged again. "I don't really know."

"You do know that you have friends, Adam. People who are willing to help you." She wanted to say Mark was one of them, but at the same time knew it was not her place.

"Yeah, I guess." Then he frowned at her. "Can I ask you something?"

"Of course."

He glanced over his shoulder as if to check whether anyone else was around. "What's up with this Chatty Mattie lady?"

"Chatty Mattie?" Alice suppressed a giggle.

He nodded. "Yeah, she never stops talking. Anyway, she's like all glommed onto Mark now. I just wondered what was up with it."

"Have you asked Mark?"

He shook his head. "I thought I better not rock his boat."

She quickly explained that they had run into Mattie and that Alice had invited her to visit.

"I don't mean to be rude, but that wasn't such a bright move on your part."

She smiled. "Why's that?"

"Well, I thought you and Mark were like a couple, you know? Now this Chatty Mattie is making the move on him." He sighed. "If it were up to me, I'd get rid of her ASAP."

"That wouldn't be very hospitable."

"Maybe not, but it would be smart."

"I was just going to check on her now," admitted Alice. "The truth is I haven't been very hospitable already."

He grinned. "Way to go."

"See you at dinner," she said, smiling in spite of herself as she headed to the parlor. As odd as that conversation had been, it was strangely comforting.

"Oh, there you are," said Mattie when Alice walked into the parlor. "I thought you'd disappeared off the planet."

"Just took a little rest." Alice sat down in the easy chair across from Mattie. "I hope you didn't feel neglected."

Mattie sat up and patted her hair. "Not at all. Mark took excellent care of me. I just hope I didn't wear the poor man out. I know that his arm is still hurting." She looked toward the doorway. "Where is he anyway?"

"I believe he went upstairs."

Mattie nodded. "I'll just freshen up a bit before dinner. I'm sure I must look a fright."

Alice assured Mattie that she still looked fine, and then showed her to the downstairs bathroom. "Dinner will be at seven," she told her.

"Goodness," said Mattie, clutching her purse. "I hope I can pull myself together by then."

❧

As always, dinner was excellent, but Alice was not so sure about the company. Mattie dominated the conversation, and many of her comments and questions seemed focused directly at Mark. Louise and Jane tried to chime in occasionally, but Alice felt mostly invisible. She noticed that Adam seemed rather quiet too. She hoped he was not slipping back into his moodiness again. Finally, the meal came to an end, and Alice rose and began to clear the table.

"I can help," offered Adam.

She tried not to register surprise as she accepted his offer, telling Jane and Louise just to sit.

"Thanks," she told him as they set the empty dishes on the counter.

"I just wanted to get out of there," he confessed, "away from Chatty Mattie. I was afraid I was going to leap across the table and strangle her or something."

Alice tried not to laugh. "Good that you didn't."

"How can Mark stand her?"

She shrugged. "Maybe he's just being polite."

"Someone should teach her to be polite." Adam studied Alice for a moment. "I know I was mean to you, Alice, and I'm sorry now. I wish you and Mark were still together. I mean, you are way better than Chatty Mattie."

"Thanks." Alice touched his cheek, and Adam smiled shyly.

As they went back out and continued to clear the table, Alice felt a mixture of gratitude and remorse. She appreciated what Adam had said about wishing she and Mark were still a couple, but it bothered her that it appeared that they no longer were a couple.

"Are you okay?" asked Jane when only she and Alice were in the kitchen. "I mean you've been so quiet tonight."

Alice shrugged. "I guess I'm having a lot of mixed feelings."

"About Mark?"

She nodded.

"Jealous?"

"Perhaps a bit, but even more than that, I feel confused."

"You and Mark should talk."

"It's a little hard . . . with Chatty Mattie around."

Jane giggled. "Chatty Mattie?"

"That's what Adam calls her."

"That's perfect."

They had invited all the guests at the inn to join them that evening for music and dessert. Louise had selected some special Easter music to play, and it was a lovely quiet evening. Alice suspected that Mattie would have preferred something more lively, but Alice was relieved that it was subdued. She was also relieved when Mattie, concerned about the drive back to Potterston, finally excused herself from the group.

Alice, playing hostess, got up to walk Mattie to the door.

"Aren't you going to see me out too?" Mattie said to Mark.

Although he looked comfortable, all settled into an easy chair, he quickly rose to his feet and joined them.

"I've had a lovely day," said Mattie directly to Mark. "I

so appreciated your little tour of Acorn Hill. I do hope you'll let me know how it goes for you and that sweet little cottage you're considering. You have my number, right?"

"Yes, you gave it to me a couple of times," said Mark as they reached the front door.

Then Mattie reached out and hugged Alice. "Thank you, dear. Let's stay in touch."

"Of course," said Alice as they stepped apart.

Then Mattie hugged Mark. Although Alice didn't time it, she felt certain that Mark's hug was much longer than her own. "You're a dear man, Mark Graves," said Mattie when she finally released him. "Now, you be sure to call me."

He smiled and nodded, then said good-bye.

"Drive safely," called Alice as she closed the front door.

Mark sighed loudly. "Glad that's over."

She studied him. "Really?"

He nodded. "That is the most tiresome woman I have ever met."

Alice couldn't help herself. She laughed aloud.

"I'm afraid I'm completely worn out, Alice. Would you make my apologies to the others?" He rubbed his cast and sighed. "I think I'd like to turn in for the night."

"Yes, that's wise."

"And may I reserve some time to talk with you tomorrow?"

"Of course."

"After church?"

"Certainly."

"Good night, Alice." He smiled warmly.

"Good night, Mark."

Chapter  Twenty-Six

The Grace Chapel Easter service was touching and uplifting. Of course, the focus was on the cross, forgiveness, redemption and grace, but for some reason Alice got the feeling that Pastor Ken had prepared his message with Mark and Adam in mind.

"God is truly the great heavenly Father," said the pastor as he finished his sermon. "He was willing to sacrifice His beloved Son in order to adopt us as His very own children. God loved us enough to give up what was incredibly precious in order to make us part of His family. And that, dear friends, is why we have reason to celebrate today."

Not for the first time, Alice thought that her father would have heartily approved of the young pastor who had taken over after his death. Although the two men were different in many ways, they shared spiritually timeless ideals and philosophy.

"That was a great sermon," said Mark as they stood outside the church afterward.

"Do you think Adam liked it?" asked Alice as she watched Adam and Laura quietly conversing.

"I actually saw him wipe a tear from his eye," said Mark.

"He really seems like a changed person," said Alice. "I think God is at work in him."

"I hope so." Mark frowned into the sunlight. "I told Adam that you and I were going to spend some time together this afternoon. Would you like to go have some lunch or do you and your sisters already have plans?"

"Actually, we'd decided to give Jane the day off. She's going to Sylvia's for Easter dinner and Louise and I were going to join Aunt Ethel and Lloyd. I'm sure they'll excuse me."

"Are you certain?"

"Positive."

"I thought we could go to Potterston," he said. "There's a restaurant that I want to try."

"That sounds good," she said.

"Do you mind driving?"

"Not at all."

They talked as she drove, mostly about Adam and the general happenings at the inn during the past week.

"In some ways it feels like I've been through the wringer," Mark admitted when Alice finally parked the Range Rover in front of the restaurant.

She nodded and handed him the keys. "I know what you mean."

"I have to ask myself, what was that all about? What was it for?"

They walked in silence into the restaurant, where they were quickly seated at a window that overlooked a garden. Alice took a deep breath, willing herself to relax as she leaned back into the chair.

"How's your arm feeling?" she asked him.

"Better, I think. I didn't even have to take a pain pill today."

"That's good." She turned and looked out the window, spying a young family in their Easter finery, taking pictures among the flowers.

"I've been doing a lot of thinking," he said.

She nodded without saying anything.

"About my life . . . and about you and me . . . and about Adam."

"I can imagine."

"Something just doesn't feel quite right." He sighed. "I have to admit that, at first, I viewed Adam as an intrusion into my life. I resented his expectations of me, or even his lack of them. But somewhere along the way, despite my misgivings, something in me changed. Maybe his change of heart touched me, or perhaps even today's sermon. But I suddenly feel different about him."

"I think I know how you mean."

He sighed. "You know, I've led a fairly self-centered life, Alice. I'm sure you have no idea how selfish I am."

She smiled. "I think it's easy to be that way when you're single and without family. I know how much you've sacrificed for your work, Mark. I've heard stories about how you've risen in the middle of the night just to care for an ailing animal or one that's about to give birth. Now, really, that wasn't selfish."

"You're too gracious."

"Besides, I think everyone is selfish in some ways," she continued. "It's just the way we humans are naturally wired."

"I feel that I am ready to quit being so self-centered, Alice." He looked into her eyes. "When I came to Acorn Hill I planned to ask you to become a bigger part of my life . . ."

She looked away uncomfortably.

"But now it seems that my life is taking a totally new direction."

She looked back at him, curious.

"When Pastor Thompson spoke about God adopting us as His own children, well, I turned and glanced over at Adam, and it's as if something in me just clicked. Can you understand what I mean?"

She smiled. "I think I do."

"I felt such empathy for him, and I remembered how close I once was to his dad, and I began to care for Adam, well, almost as if he were my own son. It was quite a staggering feeling. Does that make any sense?"

"Of course it does. It's a bit like the way I feel about the girls who are in my ANGELs group. I love them almost as if they were my own."

He nodded. "Yes, but then you're like that, Alice. You are such a fine Christian example that you put the rest of us to shame."

"Oh please, don't say that. I make mistakes all the time. Believe me, I'm just as flawed as the rest."

"So there I was sitting in church and I got this very strong feeling that I was supposed to do something very specific for Adam. Almost as if God himself was speaking to my heart. Have you ever experienced anything like that?"

She nodded. "Yes, I believe I have."

"Well, it was rather amazing. I believe I'm supposed to help Adam."

She smiled. "Yes, I thought maybe that was the case."

"That's not all." He paused as if unsure how to say the next part. "I guess I just need to tell someone, to say these words out loud, Alice."

"Go ahead."

"Well, I believe I need to parent Adam." He looked at her with wide eyes. "Do you think that's strange?"

"Not at all."

He seemed relieved. "You see, all I can think about now is how I can help him, things I can do to get him on his feet again, ways I can encourage him to pull himself up, to make something of his life. In the way that a father would help his own son. Do you know what I mean?"

She nodded, eagerly. "Yes, it's as if you've adopted him in your heart, Mark."

"That's how I feel." Mark sighed and looked out the window. "I've already made so many mistakes with him. It's possible that he won't want anything to do with this."

"No, I don't think it's like that," she assured him. "I can tell that Adam really looks up to you. Taking an active part in his life, acting as his guardian might show him just how committed you really are to him."

"That kid really has potential. He just needs someone to believe in him and to help him get going."

"Yes! That's how I feel about him too. He's really a dear boy, even if he has been a bit confused and hurt by the challenges that life has given him. It was breaking my heart to see him becoming so bitter."

"I haven't spoken to him about any of this yet," continued Mark. "I mean about what I'm thinking, specifically, but what I'd like to do is to move back to Philadelphia with him. I'll help him to get things in line to go to school. At least I hope I will. He mentioned to me that he wants to be a veterinarian. If he's serious about becoming a vet, I'll do whatever it takes to get him there." He looked at Alice. "But I have no idea how much time that will take."

She smiled. "Maybe that's not important."

He reached across the table and took her hand. "But I don't want to lose you, Alice. Or your friendship."

"You don't need to worry about that, Mark."

"So you don't feel bad about this?"

She shook her head. "I feel that you're doing the right thing, Mark. To be honest, I've felt as if something's been off between us all week. I think it's simply that you should be helping Adam right now."

He smiled. "Who knows, maybe Adam will register at a college, and perhaps even get situated into a dorm, maybe even by next fall or winter. Perhaps I can still plan to relocate to Acorn Hill sometime after that. Maybe I'll be here as early as next year. Who knows?"

"God knows."

Mark nodded. "You're right, Alice. God does know."

"And it's all in His timing, right?"

"Right."

They had a nice leisurely lunch, enjoying each other's company. By the time they got back to the inn, the other guests were getting ready to leave.

"Oh, I'm so glad you got here in time to say good-bye," Mrs. Winston told Alice as she set her bag by the front door. "I was just telling your sisters how thankful we are that we picked your little inn to visit."

"It's been quite a week," said Alice.

"I think it's just what Laura needed. Even this business with Adam has turned out to be a blessing in disguise. Don't you think?"

"I do," Alice nodded.

"Right after that lovely church service, Laura told me that she's going to start taking charge of her life now."

"Isn't that wonderful."

"She said she's tired of acting like a victim." Mrs. Winston glanced up the stairs, probably to see if the rest of her family was coming yet. "I want you to know, Alice, that even though it wasn't all smooth sailing, I think everything—including Adam and, well, just everything was absolutely perfect."

Alice squeezed her hand. "I think Laura is going to be just fine."

Mrs. Winston nodded, blinking back tears. "I do too."

"Are you down there, Mom?" called Laura from the top of the stairs.

"Yes, dear."

"Adam wants to know if I can keep Boots for him," she called.

Mrs. Winston smiled. "That'd be just fine, Laura."

Laura made a happy squeal. "It's okay, Adam!"

Soon Mr. Winston, loaded down with luggage, and Laura, holding onto Adam's arm as he carried the cat carrier, were all gathered on the front porch.

"This means you have to stay in touch, Adam," said Laura.

"I know," said Adam. "I plan on it, well, once I get settled, that is. You have to keep your promise to me and learn how to use that special computer program that your dad's been telling you about. That way we can e-mail each other, and you can give me reports on how Boots is doing. That e-mail address I gave you is good until the end of the month."

Mr. Winston winked at Alice. "I'll have the program downloaded and running by tomorrow."

"What does it do?" asked Alice.

"It's specially designed for the vision impaired," he told her, "with an electronic audio voice built right into it and all kinds of other things."

"Yeah, well, it might take me a while to figure it all out," said Laura, "but I'll do my best."

Jane and the Langleys came out onto the porch to join them. Jane had two rather large bags in her hands. "I'm helping Mr. Langley load his car," she said. "Just to prevent him from reinjuring his back."

"Oh, I'm sure I'll be fine," he said.

Alice reached over and took the one bag Mr. Langley was carrying. "Well, just in case, let us help you."

Soon all the guests had their cars loaded, and everyone was saying good-bye, giving hugs all around.

"I feel like I'm going home after a happy time spent at summer camp," said Mrs. Langley, "saying good-bye to all my new friends."

"That's how it is at Grace Chapel Inn," said Mark. "You spend a little time here and the next thing you know, you want to make it your home."

First, the Langleys, then the Winstons departed, leaving Mark, Adam and the sisters standing on the sidewalk.

"I just told Adam about my idea," said Mark as he set his good hand on Adam's shoulder.

"Yeah, if it's okay with you guys," said Adam, "I'll leave my car parked in the back of the inn for a few days." He made a face. "I know it's an eyesore. Maybe I could throw a tarp over it or—"

"No, no," said Louise. "Don't you worry about that."

Adam nodded. "I'll drive Mark back to Philadelphia today."

"When my arm's better, we'll both drive back here and pick up the Nissan," said Mark. "If that's okay."

"It's fine," Jane reassured him.

"Thanks for everything," said Adam. "I'm sorry I was such a jerk."

Jane gave him a hug. "Hey, you're a kid. It's what you do."

He smiled.

"You are always welcome here," said Louise. "Both of you."

Alice nodded. "You're like part of the family now."

They all hugged again, with Mark taking care to hug Alice last. "Thanks for being so understanding," he whispered, "and for being you."

She smiled at him.

"You take it easy on your way home," said Jane.

"Drive carefully, Adam," warned Louise.

"Take care," called Alice as she waved. *Of each other*, she thought.

After the Range Rover drove—slowly—out of sight, the sisters went up to the porch to relax.

Alice sighed as she sank down on the porch swing. "We certainly have a good life, don't we?"

"We do," agreed Jane wholeheartedly.

"And we don't have any guests until next weekend," said Louise.

"*Ah . . .*" Alice leaned back, pausing from her swinging just long enough for Wendell to pounce into her ready lap.

"A much deserved break," said Jane as she looked out across the yard.

"I made some lemonade after church," said Louise. "Would you two care for some?"

"And there are still some chocolate eggs left over," said Jane.

"I feel like I'm in heaven," said Alice as she happily stroked Wendell's soft coat. While her sisters went off to get their afternoon treat, Alice thanked God for everything, but mostly for His perfect timing.

Scalloped Potatoes with
Sweet Marjoram and Parmesan Cheese
EIGHT TO TWELVE SERVINGS

∞

½ cup plus 2 tablespoons freshly grated
  Parmesan cheese
1 tablespoon dried whole marjoram
1 teaspoon salt
½ teaspoon garlic powder
¼ teaspoon grated nutmeg
¼ teaspoon ground pepper
4 large baking potatoes (3 pounds), peeled
  and sliced thin
2 cups heavy cream
½ cup water
Parsley sprigs for garnish

Preheat oven to 350 degrees.

Combine ½ cup Parmesan cheese and next five
ingredients in a bowl.

Layer one-third of the potatoes in lightly buttered
baking dish (12" x 8" x 2"). Sprinkle half of the seasoning mixture over the potatoes. Repeat layers of potatoes
and seasonings, ending with potatoes.

Sprinkle with two tablespoons of Parmesan cheese.

Combine whipping cream and water, and pour over
potatoes.

Cover with foil and bake for one and a half hours.
Uncover and bake thirty minutes. Let stand ten minutes before serving.

Garnish with parsley.

About the Author

Melody Carlson is the author of numerous books for children, teens and adults—with sales totaling more than two million copies. She has two grown sons and lives in central Oregon with her husband and a chocolate Labrador retriever.